Other books by Annette Mahon:

The *Secret Romance* Series:

THE SECRET CORRESPONDENCE

THE SECRET CORRESPONDENCE

•

Annette Mahon

WITHDRAWAL

AVALON BOOKS
NEW YORK

Published by Thomas Bouregy & Co., Inc.
160 Madison Avenue, New York, NY 10016

Library of Congress Cataloging-in-Publication Data
    Mahon, Annette.
The secret correspondence / Annette Mahon.
        p.   cm.
    ISBN 978-0-8034-9893-8 (hardcover : acid-free paper)
1. Female friendship—Fiction.   2. Hawaii—Fiction.
3. New York (State)—Fiction.   I. Title.

    PS3563.A3595S434 2008
813'.54—dc22   2007047291

PRINTED IN THE UNITED STATES OF AMERICA
ON ACID-FREE PAPER
BY HADDON CRAFTSMEN, BLOOMSBURG, PENNSYLVANIA

This book is dedicated to pen pals,
whether the old-fashioned letter writers,
or the newer email ones.
I've enjoyed doing both.

Chapter One

It all began on a warm, dry April Monday in Malino, Hawaii. The sun shone brightly on the quiet town and the green mountains beyond. White caps dotted the long expanse of rippling green-blue ocean, and an ambulance proceeded, without the aid of its siren, to the local hospital.

In Syracuse, New York, the scene was dramatically different. Ned Smith, CPA, left his office early on Tuesday, April fifth. The snow that began falling on Monday evening showed no sign of stopping and the forecast was dire. He loaded his briefcase with everything he needed, drove to his two story town house, and unloaded it all on the desk in his home office. Inside, all was warm and efficient; outside, fat white flakes continued to blow past the window as the afternoon turned to night.

Ned worked until past nine. As he finished up for the evening, he checked online for the following day's weather forecast.

"I'll probably have to work at home," he muttered, as he scanned the information provided. What amounted to a mini-blizzard was hitting the central New York area and would probably not let up until the following afternoon.

Just before Ned turned off his computer, he decided on a last check of email. If he cleared out the spam at the end of the day, there was much less the following morning. With quick clicks, he deleted the messages offering cheap prescription drugs and golden stock opportunities. His hand stilled, though, when he came to the subject line *From your mom's neighbor.* Were the spammers getting more imaginative?

Confirming that the email did indeed come from a server in Hawaii, Ned clicked it open. Worry niggled at him, mixed with guilt. It wasn't his fault his mother decided to retire so far away, but he still couldn't help feeling he should be doing more for her.

To: Ned.smith
From: j_wong
Subj: From your Mom's neighbor

Aloha, Ned. You don't know me, but I live next door to your mom. She's a wonderful lady, one of the sweetest people I know. I hope you realize though, that she is the type who never wants to worry anyone, even when a little concern might be warranted.

Ned frowned at the screen. J_wong apparently did know his mother; the description was apt.

His eyes returned to the screen.

I hope I'm not worrying you now, because she's fine, she really is.

Ned ran his fingers through his hair. There was nothing like reassurances *not* to worry to get a body thinking that something was seriously awry.

However she did injure herself yesterday, and she's determined not to tell you—because 'it's his busy time of year and I don't want to distract him or worry him.' I had to debate with myself whether or not to get in touch. My family lives next door and she'd given us contact information some time ago—just in case of an emergency.

The tightness in Ned's chest refused to go away, even though he tried to tell himself that a true emergency would merit a phone call.

After some consideration, I've decided this is somewhat of an emergency; because I'm afraid you might be very upset with her if you don't hear anything at all until long after the fact. And it

*seems apparent to me that waiting the two weeks
until the tax season is over to tell you everything
will be too late. Your mom will be okay—there's no
doubt of that—but I feel strongly that her family
has a right to know what's happening in a timely
manner. Please pretend that I didn't contact you. I
don't want to upset your mom, and since she's now
staying at the facility where I work, this is a bit
delicate.*

Impatient now, and still concerned, Ned scanned the
paragraphs ahead. Relieved at what he saw, he went
back to read it more slowly.

*So, this is to tell you that yesterday, your mom
tripped over Ginger (and she is* so *embarrassed
about that) and broke her leg.*

He had a sudden vision of his mother stumbling over
the prone body of a red-headed woman. Until he recalled that Ginger was the name of the dog his mother
had inherited from her old friend.

*She managed to get to the phone and call 9-1-1 on
her own, and she now has a heavy cast on her right
leg. And crutches. The doctor insisted that she have
a short stay at the care center where I work. This is
a multi-purpose facility that includes assisted living quarters as well as a restorative care wing for
patients like your mom who are recovering from*

surgery or illness. *Her doctor worried about her being alone in the house with Ginger; with the cast on and crutches, he thought it would be difficult for her to manage everyday tasks and felt she could trip again, causing a more serious injury.*

That said, your mom is not too happy, because she doesn't want to 'be a bother.' Actually, I'm rather surprised that she came here and didn't just tell the doctor she was going home, period. She's a competent adult, so she can decide on her treatment, but you are her only relative and I feel you should be informed about what's happening.

So, I guess that's it. Please, please don't contact your Mom right away and yell at her for being clumsy or something. Or call and yell at me for not abiding by her wishes. I hope I read you correctly. With a mother like yours, I figure you have to be a good guy. So I hope you live up to my ideal of you. :-)

Aloha, Julie Wong

While Ned was checking his email in Syracuse, in Malino, Julie Wong walked into The Hair Place to meet her friend Abby for their Tuesday evening exercise class. Hair stylist Abby Andrews had started the group upon returning to Malino after years in LA. Abby hated to exercise alone, so she lost no time recruiting Julie to join her. Abby's bubbly personality and the chance to keep in shape right there in their tiny town quickly attracted enough other young women to outgrow the space available at the salon. They now met at a nearby church, which allowed them free use of a larger room.

"Julie, you look exhausted." Abby grasped her best friend in a bear hug, holding her close for a moment while her small dog danced around their feet. "Are you feeling okay?"

"Yes." Julie returned the hug, then dropped to the floor to greet Mano. Once the pup was properly fussed over, and Julie's face well licked, she plopped down on the sofa, stretching her feet out in front of her. She dreaded the coming workout, though she felt sure she'd appreciate it later. And she *really* wanted to talk to Abby. "I am tired. It's been an exhausting day. I probably shouldn't have come."

"You'll feel better afterward," Abby said, confirming Julie's thought.

"That's what I've been telling myself," Julie muttered.

"So what happened to tire you out so much?" Abby sat in an overstuffed chair beside the sofa and Mano leaped into her lap.

"You know Mrs. Smith, our neighbor?"

Abby nodded, a smile brightening her pretty face. "The one with the same name as her pen pal, your late aunt?"

"I guess there are no secrets from the town's hair stylist, huh?" Julie matched her smile.

Sometimes it seemed amazing that Abby had only been back in town for a year. She'd moved to LA with her parents at the age of twelve and only returned a year ago. They'd been best friends in grade school, and once she came back, it was as though they'd never been apart.

"Aunty Claudia used to talk about her all the time," Julie said. "Her *haole* pen pal with the same name— until they both married of course."

Claudia Lee Smith and Claudia Lee Azevedo had been pen pals from the age of ten, when Claudia Lee of Malino—of Hawaiian, Chinese, Portuguese, Scotch and Spanish ancestry—found the other girl's name in a newspaper pen pal column and decided to write to her. She couldn't believe there was another Claudia Lee, just her age—but of English and German descent— living in Syracuse, New York.

"Mrs. Smith moved here right about the time I did," Abby said.

After some fifty years of corresponding, both women became widows within a year of each other, and Malino Claudia invited Syracuse Claudia to share her home. Sadly, Julie's Aunty Claudia died of a sudden and totally unexpected stroke a mere six months after her new housemate's arrival. She'd left the house to her only child, a son who was a doctor in Honolulu, but stipulated that Mrs. Smith could live there for her lifetime.

"It's such a shame they didn't have more time together," Abby added.

Julie nodded. "I still miss my Aunty Claudia, but it's nice having Mrs. Smith there. I don't miss Aunty quite as much with the other Claudia around."

Abby nodded her understanding. "Did something happen to Mrs. Smith?"

"She fell and broke her leg. I happened to be home for lunch and got quite a scare when I saw the ambulance. It was like Aunty Claudia all over again." She sighed, remembering the shock surrounding her aunt's sudden death.

"Is she okay?"

"She's fine. Can you believe it—she tripped over Ginger."

Ginger was her Aunty Claudia's beloved Golden Retriever, who was also provided for in her will. Like Claudia Smith, Ginger got to live in the house for her lifetime.

"Oh, dear." Abby looked down at Mano, curled up on the seat beside her and staring up at her with adoring eyes. "I can see how it could happen, though, especially with a big dog like Ginger. Mano gets underfoot a lot, but he's a little guy. It's more likely that he'd be the one to get hurt if I tripped over him."

Julie frowned. "I wonder if a Golden Retriever is too active for a small woman like Mrs. Smith. Ginger is almost ten, but she still acts like a puppy sometimes. Mrs. Smith is only sixty-two, but she looks older, don't you think? And I've never seen her do anything active."

Abby nodded. "I tried to talk her into coloring her hair when she first came in for a trim. She said her hair was the color of those golden brown mums you see in the fall. She seemed quite proud of it. Still, she wouldn't let me color it for her." Abby shook her head, amazed at anyone who would neglect their crowning glory. "She has beautiful skin and would look much younger if she let me dye her hair golden brown again. But she said she didn't want to bother with it."

Julie sighed. "That's her all right. She never wants to be a bother to anyone. I guess not to herself either."

"I don't think she approved of *my* hair."

Julie grinned. When Abby first arrived in Malino, her short brown hair with its purple-tinted highlights was a subject of much discussion among the townsfolk. For the most part, the young people liked it and thought Abby very trendy. The *makuas,* the older ladies, clicked their tongues and spoke of the dangers of Hollywood living.

"What color was it that week?" Since she'd opened the refurbished salon, Abby had tended toward more "normal" hair colors. She still wore a short, trendy style, but now her highlights ran mainly to gold or red.

Abby shrugged. "I don't recall."

Abby never apologized for her hair color. Luckily, her new fiancé found her hair "interesting," and often said he missed the original purple.

"Must have been during your orange period." Julie couldn't suppress a giggle.

Abby swiftly changed the subject. "So what happened? Did she call you when she fell?"

"No, she called nine-one-one. I was in the kitchen having lunch and heard the siren. I followed them to the hospital with some things for Mrs. Smith, in case she had to stay over, you know? Anyway, she has a cast on her right leg and she moved into the restorative care part of the facility this morning. She's as sweet as pie, and constantly worrying that she'll be a burden on someone." Julie sighed. "She insisted that I wasn't to notify her son on the mainland."

Apparently hearing something in her tone, Abby's eyebrows lifted. "And did you call him anyway?"

"Not exactly." Julie shifted uncomfortably on the sofa. It still bothered her that she'd gone against her neighbor's wishes. "I emailed him." Her mouth pulled down in a sardonic frown. "It's not calling, but I know it's not what she wanted." She turned pleading eyes toward Abby. "But it bothered me terribly that she was suffering and her only living relative didn't know anything about it."

"She talked about her son when I cut her hair. She said he was a nice son but that he's rather dull." Abby shook her head. "Isn't that an odd thing for a mother to say about her son?"

Julie shrugged. "He's an accountant," she said. "She's proud about that. I've seen a photo of him, and he's absolutely gorgeous. Too much to hope he'd be a great date too, I guess."

Abby scooted Mano off the chair as she stood, gesturing to Julie that it was time to go. "Maybe it's genetic. Mrs. Smith is a bit on the dull side herself."

"Tell me about it. I knew she was shy, so I worried that she would retreat into herself and spend her time sitting in a corner with a book or some knitting. It's happened before."

Julie shook her head as she rose from the sofa. She couldn't have been more wrong. "But you should have seen her." Her eyes glowed as she recalled Mrs. Smith's arrival at the Hale.

Abby was puzzled. "What happened? She suddenly turned into an extrovert?"

"Almost." Julie's voice was touched with amusement. "It was the strangest thing. She didn't want to stay at the Hale. I heard her myself at the hospital, telling the doctor that she wanted to go home. When I went to pick her up, I thought she looked almost afraid. Then the residents from the assisted living area of the Hale welcomed her with leis and a little party of punch and cookies. Mrs. Akaka told her how nice it was to have such a young person staying. And it was like a connection was made. She and Mrs. Akaka became instant friends."

Abby nodded. "Mrs. Akaka is just the opposite of Mrs. Smith. I could see how they might make a good pair."

"You should have been there," Julie said. "It was like a mutual admiration society. Mrs. Akaka told her she was going to be one hundred in two weeks and Mrs. Smith asked about her secret for such a long life, and they were off and running." Julie grabbed her exercise bag, slinging the straps over her shoulder.

"I can just hear her," Abby said. "Probably told her she enjoyed life to the fullest."

Julie grinned. "Pretty much. She told her it was important to do things, to have fun, and to laugh."

"What good advice," Abby said. "We do that, don't we, Mano?"

Mano responded by cocking his ears and wagging his tail. The two women laughed.

"Then the most amazing thing happened," Julie continued, ignoring the interruption. "When she mentioned doing things and having fun, Mrs. Smith asked if anyone played the piano. You know we have that upright piano in the sun room."

"And does anyone play?" Abby asked, opening the door for Julie.

"Not at the moment. Sometimes someone comes in, from a church or a school group," Julie said, while Abby locked the salon door. "But here's the amazing part. Mrs. Smith says 'I play,' and tells me to take her over to the piano—she was in a wheelchair. And she starts playing, without sheet music." Julie laughed at the memory. "She played these old show tunes, and everyone sang along. They had the best time. It's going to be great fun for everyone, having Mrs. Smith at the Hale. Especially for her . . ."

Julie continued talking as they walked the short distance to the church. "I have a feeling she thought the Hale Maika'i would be like a nursing home in a made-for-TV movie—filled with elderly people sitting in front of a television all day, unaware of what's happening around them. A lot of people think that. I've lost count of the number of people who ask me how I can stand to work there and 'isn't it just totally depressing' because they have the same picture in their minds."

"I thought the same thing before I went over there," Abby admitted. She'd first visited the Hale Maika'i for

Mrs. Akaka's ninety-ninth birthday, offering to fix the residents' hair for the party. She'd enjoyed the women there, and made it a tradition to visit whenever any of them celebrated a birthday, donating her time and talent to fix the women's hair.

"Don't mention to anyone that I contacted her son," Julie said as they walked up the path to the church auxiliary building.

Abby dismissed the request with a quick wave of her hand. "Of course not."

But despite her friend's support, Julie continued to fret while Abby got things set up. Her unorthodox action could be construed as unethical. Biting her lip in agitation, she told herself once again that it was the right thing to do. Especially when it concerned a friend like their neighbor. *Surely her only living relative should know what was happening. Could he sue the facility if they kept the news from him? Could Claudia sue them for not keeping it private? Would they both sue her for interfering?*

Julie didn't resolve her problem in the five minutes before class started, but she was sure of one thing. No matter the reaction of Ned Smith, she'd done what her heart dictated.

Ned's brows furrowed as he reread the email from his mother's neighbor. He wavered between concern over his mother, and a mixture of feelings about Julie Wong. Who was this person who had taken it unto herself to inform him of things Claudia preferred to keep private?

While he appreciated learning about his mother's accident, two weeks before April fifteenth things were hectic enough without having his mother to worry about. He knew that was why his mother preferred to keep the news from him, and he could sympathize.

But a smile came unbidden to his lips when Ms. Wong called him "a good guy." He suspected that the meddlesome neighbor was trying to scold him into living up to her descriptive—or guilt him into it.

Ned sighed. Unfortunately, this sounded exactly like something Claudia Lee Smith would do. She constantly worried that she would be a "bother." It was a word he had tired of early in life. Even when his father died some two years ago, she was concerned that she might be a burden on others. Although he and her friends offered to help out, she ended up doing almost everything herself. It was her way.

It shocked him to his heels when she decided to leave her lifetime home in Syracuse and move to a tiny town in Hawaii. Fiercely independent, his mother was a shy woman who was active in the various women's groups at their church. During his school years, she volunteered with the PTA. She entertained his father's business associates and visited with the neighbors when they were outdoors. But she'd never had any close friendships that he could remember.—Except with her pen pal. Maybe he should have expected her to join this one special friend, although he hadn't seen it coming.

And now she was alone in a tiny town thousands of miles from her lifelong home. She was sixty-two and in good health, as far as he knew. Apart from this broken leg.

His first impulse was to pick up the phone and call. To hear for himself that she was okay and relieve his mind at the same time.

A quick glance at the clock told him it was late afternoon in Hawaii. He picked up the phone, ready to punch in the numbers, when he realized that he *couldn't* call. His mother wasn't at home and he didn't have a number for the facility.

He skimmed over the email from Ms. Wong. There was no mention of the care center name. She probably didn't want him to call and get her into trouble. He'd wanted to get his mother a cell phone for a Christmas gift, but she'd said she didn't want one, that it would be too complicated for an old woman like her.

Ned took a deep breath and sighed. Of all times for this to happen. As a CPA specializing in tax services, the first part of the year was his busiest. And these first two weeks in April were crazy. He barely had time to spare, even for decent meals, until after April fifteenth. In fact, he couldn't remember if he'd eaten when he got home that day. A perfectly timed rumble from his midsection told him he must have forgotten.

With another sigh, he pushed himself away from his desk and went down to the kitchen. Snow had drifted halfway up his sliding doors and he could see that it was still coming down. The wind seemed to have lessened, but fat flakes continued to drift down, visible in the lights that illuminated the parklike common area beyond.

Ned took a prepared meal from the freezer and tore open the box. As he set the timer on the microwave he thought about a Hawaiian vacation. Sun, sand and a visit with his mother—to be sure she was recovering okay. It sounded darned good. It was Tuesday, April fifth. He could leave on Saturday, the sixteenth. Many of the CPAs he knew took off on the sixteenth. He'd actually mentioned something of the kind when he talked to his mother during their Christmas phone call— vaguely mentioning a visit after tax season. But, in typical fashion, she had not pursued the suggestion.

Ned had yet to see his mother's island home. She'd moved a year ago, during his usual hectic spring season, prompting him to wonder if she'd planned it that way. So that her moving wouldn't be a bother to him. He tried not to interfere in her life, but if he hadn't been so busy, he would have attempted to convince her to stay in the area where she'd spent her entire life. Where she knew everyone at the church she'd belonged to since before his birth, and the woman next door had been her neighbor for twenty years.

Then her new roommate had died suddenly in the fall, when he'd been in the midst of a personal crisis involving his partner and his extremely messy divorce, a divorce that included accusations against Ned by the soon-to-be ex-wife. Unfounded accusations, but enough to almost achieve her spiteful purpose—a rift between the two old friends and their business partnership. Claudia had told him in no uncertain terms that she would be fine, and he was to take care to clear his good name. So he still had not seen her in her new home.

Since the new year, his weekly calls had been brief; he had less and less time to spare for anything other than business. The proposed vacation had not been mentioned again. He didn't know if she wasn't interested in seeing him, or if she just didn't want to bother him by bringing it up. Probably the latter.

The microwave beeped and he removed his dinner. Still shaking his head over his mother and the impossibility of deciphering her thought processes, he reached into the refrigerator for a beer. He deserved one while he figured out what to do. A flick of the remote and smooth jazz filled the apartment. If not for the dilemma of his mother's neighbor, it would have been a relaxing twenty minutes eating his dinner and listening to Norman Brown.

Afterward, he returned to his computer and re-read the note from Julie Wong. Had his mother ever mentioned the name? A neighbor she said. Then he remembered that the other Claudia had a sister who lived next door. That must be who this Julie was. She did seem sincere, the way a relative of her dear friend might. He pictured a woman about his mother's age, salt-and-pepper hair cut short and neatly arranged in some nondescript style. Someone whose life was so dull she was more interested in the lives of those around her—a mother hen working in a care center and looking out for her temporary patients.

Cupping his hand over the mouse, he decided to reply to the email and see what developed. Tomorrow he'd try to figure out just where this care center was and how to get in touch—as soon as he could find time during his hectic day to search it on the internet.

Manipulating the mouse with quick sure stokes, he clicked on REPLY and began to type.

Julie was relieved when Abby began the workout music. It meant she wouldn't have to think for the next forty minutes.

But soon enough the session was over and she was helping Abby put away her sound equipment before following her outside.

"So what did your email accomplish?" Abby asked, as they walked slowly back toward The Hair Place. "Was he mad at you? Or at his mother?"

"I haven't heard back yet. That's why I'm a nervous wreck. At least if he replied, even if he yelled at me . . ." At Abby's raised brows, she shrugged; she supposed it was odd to say someone could yell at her in an email, but then he could send a message all in caps. "You know what I mean. But at least I'd *know*."

"You're just excited about hearing from some good-looking guy with a steady job."

Julie started to deny it, then laughed instead. Her cheeks grew pink. "Well, maybe a little. Everyone who's seen that photo in Mrs. Smith's family room has exclaimed over his looks. You sure don't meet guys like that in Malino."

Abby raised her brows. "Oh, I don't know. Kevin is very handsome."

"Yeah, but he's taken," Julie replied.

As they approached The Hair Place, Abby gestured across the street, where the Dairy Queen lights glowed in the early evening gloom. "Want to go have a burger?"

"Yeah, why not?" Julie laughed. "After all, I just did all that exercising. I guess I can have some greasy fries."

"Comfort food," Abby declared.

Chapter Two

Julie arrived home pleasantly tired from her exercise session and excited because Abby had used their interlude at the Dairy Queen to ask Julie to be her maid of honor. After sharing that news with Julie parents, she took Ginger outside for a short romp then soaked in a leisurely bath. But even her favorite gardenia-scented bath crystals couldn't relieve her concern about Ned and his possible reaction to her message.

When she got out of the tub, she pulled on her pajamas and went straight to the computer. She could check for messages at her work address from home, and she planned to do so now. Unaware of holding her breath, Julie pulled up her messages. Her eyes scanned the row of subject lines, quickly weeding out the ones that announced she'd *already won* or reminded her of non-existent appointments.

Her breath flew out in a swoosh when she saw what she was looking for. *Re: From your Mom's neighbor.* He'd answered her!

Sitting up a little straighter in her chair, Julie clicked the message open. Butterflies seemed to have taken up residence in her midsection as she glanced at the brief message.

To: j_wong
From: Ned.smith
Subj: Re: From your Mom's neighbor

Ms. Wong:

Thank you for keeping me apprised re Mother's condition. Your description sounds exactly like Mother, i.e. she never wants to be a bother. I'll agree to keeping your communication private. For the time being. It would be impossible for me to get away at the moment, although I would like to talk to her. However, I have no way to contact her at this time. I usually call on Sunday evening— that would be at noon your time—so she'll have to let me know before then if she won't be at home. Or will she return by then?

Ned Smith

Julie read the succinct note, then read it again. He seemed so formal, so cold. Mrs. Smith had said that he was an accountant, and busy at this time of year. Too busy to take time off to see her. Still, she did seem to think that he would fly out if he heard about her injury, so that was a point in his favor. And he did agree to keeping their correspondence a secret, so she supposed that was another plus.

Julie read it through a third time. "Keeping me apprised"? "Mother's condition"? "Mother"?

Her small nose crinkled in disgust at the pompous phrasing. From an English literature professor, maybe, but a CPA? He was so handsome in that photo at Claudia's, with a playful smile teasing his lips. She'd expected something warmer, perhaps even a touch of humor.

She sighed. Well, he'd thanked her, and he didn't threaten to inform her superiors about going against his mother's wishes. Still, she wished he was—what? More like her expectations, she supposed.

Her cell phone rang. Still busy digesting the post, Julie almost ignored it. Until she realized it must be Abby, calling to see if she'd heard from Ned. Caller ID confirmed it.

"Abby," she began, before her friend even had time to say hello. "He answered."

"And . . ." Abby prompted.

"Well, it's going to be okay, I think. He doesn't sound mad."

"You don't sound sure," Abby said.

Abby knew her too well, Julie thought. "No, I'm sure he isn't mad. But I can't get much of an impression of what he's like from his reply. It's very curt and busi-nesslike."

"Really?"

"It would be funny if it wasn't so sad. In Mrs. Smith's photo, he's so handsome, with this smile ready to burst out. I just can't believe this is the same man. He thanks me for 'keeping him apprised.' Can you imag-ine? And he calls her 'Mother'."

"Really, he calls her Mother? Yikes." Then she gig-gled. "He really said *apprised*?"

Julie gave a bark of laughter. "That's pretty much what I thought. I've been sitting here staring at the computer screen trying to think of how to reply."

"You just be your usual warm, friendly self, and tell him how his mother's doing."

Julie offered a silent prayer for good friends.

"Thanks for that. I think I'll wait until morning to re-ply. It's the middle of the night in Syracuse anyway."

"Good idea. Get a good night's sleep," Abby advised. "You'll know what to say when you wake up."

Julie said good-bye and turned off the computer. Abby was right; she'd think of a way to answer in the morning. She just wished she could find something in Ned's email that made him seem like a real person. It was too impersonal, much too cold for her taste. And was he scolding her there at the end—saying he had no way to contact her? Was he implying that she should have included contact information for the care center?

Julie climbed into bed, plumping the pillows up

against the headboard and reaching for the romance novel on her bedside table. Right now the thought of escaping into the fantasy world of Regency England held a lot of appeal; the dashing hero in its pages held more allure than continued thoughts of Mr. Ned Smith. Even if Ned was better looking than the gentleman pictured on the book cover.

Ned awoke on Wednesday morning to over two feet of snow but clearing skies. He had a late morning appointment with a client, and the snow plow hadn't reached his street yet. He decided to start the morning's work at home.

As he sat in front of his computer, Ned remembered the email from Julie Wong and looked through his mail folder for a reply. Nothing.

He checked his watch and made a quick calculation. It was the middle of the night in Hawaii. If she hadn't sent a reply last night—and it didn't look like she had—he'd have to wait until the afternoon at the earliest. The six-hour time difference made communication between Syracuse and Malino tricky at best. It was a shame they'd just gone on daylight savings time—even that one hour difference could make it easier.

Pushing aside thoughts of his mother and her strange neighbor, Ned went to work.

Julie knew she had to answer Ned's email. So, as soon as she arrived at her office on Wednesday morning, she pulled up his message. A third reading did not tell her anything more about the sender than her first two the night before. With a sigh, she hit REPLY. She would tell him about the warm welcome his mother had received.

Julie paused, her fingers hovering above the keyboard, before she began a recounting of the welcome party and Claudia's delight in it. She told him how his mother seemed to come out of her shell when she met one of the other residents and formed an instant friendship. She finished with a few words about Claudia's medical condition and signed off.

Just in time.

Julie heard the squeak of a rubber–soled shoe on the hall floor and one of the residents appeared in her doorway. Not Mrs. Smith, thank goodness.

"Julie, do you still have the supplies for the Hawaiian quilting?"

"The patterns and squares of fabric? Sure. I'll get them for you."

Breathing a sigh of relief that she'd already closed her mail window, she led Mrs. Milho to the storage cupboard. She couldn't wait for Mrs. Smith to talk to her son. The guilt of her secret correspondence was already getting to her.

Ned managed an actual lunch on Wednesday; the roads were cleared in time for his late-morning appointment, who had a deli lunch catered in. The meal was better than he'd hoped, the meeting lasted longer than he'd planned but resolved several issues, and he returned to the office late.

Numerous messages had accumulated in the twenty-four hours since he'd last been in. He sorted through it all quickly—until he found the latest note from Julie Wong. Although he knew she would hate being in a care center, he was happy to know that his mother would not be at home alone. If she fell over the dog when she was not hampered by crutches and a clumsy cast, heaven knew what could happen now.

As he read Julie's recounting of his mother's welcome to the care center, he grew increasingly astonished. He barely recognized the woman she spoke of, who formed instant friendships and played sing-a-long songs on the piano.

She'd played the piano, he thought with wonder.

Ned stared across the room, not seeing the polished oak of the door or the print hanging on the wall beside it. He'd almost forgotten that she played. What memories that brought . . .

Ned blinked a few times, clearing his mind. He had a lot of work to do, too much to afford time for nostalgic recollections.

He returned to the lengthy email, glancing at the clock and back. Did he really have time for this indulgence?

It was his mother, he reminded himself. Of course he had time.

Your mother is doing well and having daily physical therapy. The doctor didn't want her to be alone at home without some training in how to manage with the crutches, etc. He also thought it advisable to start her on an exercise regime.

We have Ginger at our house and she's happy enough. Whenever I take her outside, though, I can see her look over toward her own home. I think she's looking for your mom. Poor thing, it hasn't been that long since she lost her previous owner. I still miss my Aunty Claudia but it's very nice to have her lifelong friend here near us. It helps fill the void left by her death that the house isn't cold and empty, or filled with strangers.

We miss your mom in the neighborhood, and look forward to having her back, better than before.

He reread the last few lines. Her Aunty Claudia. He redrew his mental picture of his new correspondent. A bleeding heart type, but younger than his initial image. Much younger. Was that how she was drawing out his mother? Youth often had a remarkable effect on old people.

Not that his mother was very old, he reminded himself. Sixty-two was far from old in the twenty-first century. She merely projected old in her demeanor because of poor posture and a marked indifference to hair dye, cosmetics, and current fashion. Perhaps this experience at the care center was just what she needed to make her see that she was *not* an old woman.

He sent a brief reply thanking Julie for the update and asking that she keep him informed. He added a final assurance that he would not contact his mother until his usual Sunday call and signed off.

He felt a deep warmth pulse through him as he anticipated hearing from Julie Wong again. Was it just the fact that he now knew she was a young woman who cared deeply about an older woman who wasn't even a relative? Or was it her faith in him and his basic integrity?

The mornings passed quickly at the Hale Maika'i, as Julie kept busy organizing new activities or supervising ongoing ones. Around 12:30, she settled behind her desk, pulled out the sandwich she'd brought for lunch, and brought up her email to sort while she ate. She deleted three posts for online backgammon—that was something different—then, seeing a new post from Ned, eagerly opened it. A quick read through left her staring at the computer screen, her sandwich forgotten on the napkin beside her keyboard.

Ms. Wong:
Thank you for the update. Please keep me informed.
Will contact Mother on Sunday per our previous correspondence.
Sincerely, Ned Smith

Julie sighed, then picked up her sandwich and took a bite. She'd sent that long, newsy progress report hoping to draw out the man who'd come across as cold in his initial reply. She wanted to soften him, break down that brisk businesslike tone from the previous email. She wanted him to burst into that smile that hovered on his lips in Mrs. Smith's photo.

Julie sighed again. Ned barely seemed human from these two brief notes. He didn't even ask after Ginger, though of course he didn't really know the dog. And she had told him she and her family were taking care of Ginger, so she supposed there was no further reason for him to concern himself with the dog. Still, he might have expressed an interest in her care since his mother was not at home. He knew she lived alone. He knew she had a dog.

He did, didn't he? Poor Mrs. Smith seemed to be saddled with more than a boring son. Julie's molars met and her jaw set as she stared at the monitor. The man in that photograph could not be the cold, unfeeling person she was extrapolating from these messages. Well, she'd look upon it as a challenge. Somehow, she'd get to the real Ned Smith and see that he became more involved in his mother's life.

She glanced at the message again.

"Mother." Did anyone really address their parent as mother? No one she knew, that was for sure. Even Abby thought it odd, and she'd grown up in Los Angeles.

Julie began another note. She wanted him to react, to do more than return a short businesslike sentence or two. As a child, she'd never been able to resist a dare. This wasn't quite the same thing, but close enough. She'd get Ned to soften up if it was the last thing she ever did.

With a grim smile, Julie hit REPLY. She'd felt sure

he'd want to answer her last note by sharing something of himself, or some remembrance of his mother. There was ample opportunity for him to recall something of her piano playing, or to comment on the manner in which she made friends.

Once they moved past the sticky issue of her sharing supposedly private information, she'd expected him to lighten up—at least ask for details of his mother's condition, or of her rehabilitation. He didn't even inquire about her doctor wanting her to get more exercise. Should she mention the high incidence of osteoporosis in older women? The orthopedist had explained that Mrs. Smith's bones were thinner than they should be in a woman of her age. He felt it was a contributing factor in her broken leg. One of the things the Hale Maika'i staff was supervising was the taking of calcium supplements and a restructuring of her diet to include calcium-rich foods.

Julie began to type. In no time at all, she ate the final bit of her sandwich, surprised to realize that she'd finished off her entire lunch while she worked. As she disposed of the empty plastic bags and juice can, she wished she could be there when Ned read her latest missive. She'd be very interested in seeing if there would be a reply—and just what it would entail.

Ned got home from work at eight, heated a meal in the microwave, then took it up to his desk. There was still a lot he needed to do before retiring for the night and he didn't want to indulge himself. If he settled into his recliner with some good music on the stereo, he might not get up again until morning.

He thought of Julie and his mother as he plugged his laptop into its station. Momentarily, guilt pangs struck. He hadn't even tried to discover anything about the care center where his mother was staying. But even if it was a distraction he had no time for, he felt a shiver of anticipation when he spotted another email from Julie.

As he read through the beginning of the message, however, Ned wondered if Julie had mis-sent a post. He skimmed through several paragraphs about osteoporosis before finally realizing that she was telling him this was a problem for Claudia. With more interest, he backtracked to the beginning of the post and read it again. The diagnosis did not surprise him; he wondered why he had not thought of the possibility himself. He clearly remembered teasing her about shrinking, but he hadn't thought to follow up on it.

As he continued to read, Ned found himself enthralled. When Julie began to talk about the residents at the facility, he detected a deep caring in her words; he also found himself fascinated. He didn't even mind that he had hours' worth of work left before he could escape to his bed.

Although your mother was originally reluctant to spend time here at the Hale Maka'i, she is fitting in very nicely. The other women are sorry that she is here for such a short stay. They love her piano playing and have requested daily sing-a-longs. I wish you could see your mother leading them in old Broadway show tunes. The Hale hasn't been so jolly since the Christmas concerts put on by the local schools.

Jolly and Claudia Smith! It was the ultimate oxymoron, Ned thought. His shy mother, leading sing-a-longs. It boggled the mind.

And then he laughed out loud. He really wanted to meet this Julie and her friendly group of senior citizens. If they could have this effect on his mother . . .

Your mother is quite an asset to Hale Maika'i. I arrived this morning to find everyone gathered in the community room, their happiness and excitement definitely catching. They discovered that while Claudia could sew, and had even done some quilting, she didn't know about Hawaiian quilts. And they couldn't wait to teach her. I haven't seen the other residents get so involved in an activity for a long time. Even Mr. Morimoto, who is usually so quiet and withdrawn you barely know he's there, got involved. Claiming he could produce better patterns than the ones the women were sharing, he proceeded to do just that. And then he confided that he'd always wanted to paint. He'd been a gardener and I know he misses his plants and his time outdoors. We have a garden here, and the residents may work in it if they choose, but with his breathing problems he is supposed to stay inside where the air conditioner filters the air. His emphysema is so bad his doctor wanted him close to professional help 24/7. Even in this part of the island, we have intermittent problems with the vog, that can be very serious for a man in his condition. It was much worse in the area where he used to live though, which is why his daughter brought him here. Vog BTW is the local version of smog, created by the live volcano eruption.

Ned paused, going back to reread the last line. "Live volcano eruption."

Somewhere in his number cluttered brain, Ned was aware that Hawaii boasted one of the most active volcanoes in the world. Yet he'd never associated that with his mother and her residence there. Until now. Just how far *was* Malino from the live volcano?

The quilting patterns Mr. Morimoto created for the women are beautiful. In fact, I hope to interest the local quilt shop in them. He's so happy at the positive response he received. And you should see how content he is now that I have provided him with some art supplies. I called his daughter, and she is as amazed as I am. He seems ten years younger. And it's all due to your mother. She's truly a sweetheart of a person. She and Mrs. Akaka— our celebrity resident, as she turns one hundred soon—have become such friends. They are like two teenage girls, always sitting together, sharing secrets. Your mom is more like the woman who moved here a year ago. I hadn't realized until now how much she's aged since Aunty Claudia passed away. I guess losing her pen pal and friend af- fected her more than any of us could know. We did worry that she spent too much time alone, but she always said she was just fine. Her progress in just two days is already amazing, so I think by the time she checks out she will be looking and feeling years younger. She might not want to admit to a son as old as you.

Ned read Julie's newest note with a vague sense of disbelief. First he was astonished at the size of the new email. Didn't she have anything else to do? He hadn't expected more than a line or two on his mother's condition—if he heard from her at all.

As he read, however, he was drawn in by her newsy style. In addition, he was being reintroduced to his mother. The Claudia Julie described was certainly not the woman he'd been talking to these past two years. Ned loved his mother, but she was a small, quiet, self-effacing person who made little impression on most people. She was only sixty-two but looked eighty-two. Was she blossoming because of her new friendships? Or was it Julie bringing out her inner child? He looked at the screen, startled to find it filled with type. The woman did have a way of drawing people out.

Quilts.

His mother had made quilts when he was a child. He

didn't know what was particularly Hawaiian about quilting in the islands, but he clearly remembered a quilt his mother had made for him. Sailboats. At the age of eight he'd loved boats above all things, and he'd loved that quilt. Sleeping beneath it had been a pleasure.

Goodness, he hadn't thought about that for years. He wondered what had become of the old quilt. He'd used it until it became tattered, so it had probably been thrown away.

Ned blinked. He'd been staring blankly at the wall long enough for his eyes to feel dry. Still, quilting made sense, even if the other gregarious behaviors did not.

And what was that crack about his age? He wasn't old!

Frustrated at his new unfamiliarity with his mother and irritated at the way Julie intrigued him, Ned sent off the email and threw himself back into his work. Numbers were easy to understand. He knew his way around numbers and felt comfortable with them.

He forgot his mother for the next few hours. Until he prepared for bed. That's when he remembered the way his mother sang to him. Lullabies. It was such a long time ago. Julie's mention of the sing-a-longs must have triggered the memory and a snatch of melody, which brought a glow of well-being allowing him to relax. As a result, he fell asleep in a much shorter time than was usual at this busy, stress-filled time of year.

Julie was pleasantly surprised when she read the latest email from Ned on Thursday morning. Finally, he'd sent more than a line or two.

*I'm sorry to hear about Mother's osteoporosis.
While I was unaware of the problem, it does explain some things I'd noticed before she moved. So
I guess I didn't have a growth spurt at the age of
thirty-one. I'm glad to hear she has started treatment.*

A joke! He'd made a joke!

Julie smiled. Finally, he was breaking that shell that
she'd suspected hid the man in the photo. *That* man had
a happy-go-lucky side that was finally being exposed.
And, he'd revealed his age without her asking an out-
right question.

Her heart sank. If he was thirty-one when Claudia
moved a year and a half ago, he was either thirty-two or
thirty-three. Almost ten years separated them.

Then she almost slapped her own cheek, asking herself what on earth she was about, imagining that they
could be a couple. After a mere three exchanges of
emails. It must be the emotional distress she'd gone
through over the initial correspondence. Because Julie
felt as though she'd known Ned longer than that.

With a sigh she glanced back at the new message,
the one that she felt was finally revealing the real Ned.
He did sound like someone she wanted to get to know.
And she couldn't forget how handsome he was. It must
be her mother's constant hints about dating and mar-
riage that had her looking at every man as a potential
mate. Or perhaps it was just part of being female.

Her mind went back to that age difference. There

were famous couples who'd made marriages work with even more of an age difference. She searched her mind for examples, drawing a complete blank, then scolded herself for even caring. Did she actually think that she and Ned could become a couple? What a fantasy! She knew this particular day dream was just that—but it still emphasized the fact that she was alone. Her heart felt hollow as she turned her attention back to the monitor.

Just how far is Malino from the live volcano? Is there any danger, besides that from the vog? As far as I know, Mother does not suffer from respiratory problems.

Julie stopped reading for a moment. Hmm, so he was genuinely concerned about his mother's health. And he was worried about the volcanoes. It sounded so . . . mainland-ish of him. It made him seem more human. More normal.

Mother used to make quilts. She made one for me when I was a little boy. I'd almost forgotten. It was blue and white and had sailboats on it. I loved that quilt.

A warm smile graced Julie's lips. Finally, he'd opened up a bit with a personal memory.

Your recounting of her activities continues to amaze me. I find myself wondering if she has changed so much because of her move, or if you and your staff there aren't drawing her out of herself. Perhaps you are a bit of a sorceress, Ms. Julie Wong.

Mother is fiercely independent but has always been timid as well, a rather strange combination of characteristics. I fear my father's early death pushed her to more extremes of both behaviors. I still feel bad that I was unable to come for a visit last Oct when her dear friend died. I know this was your aunt, and I am sorry for your loss. I believe your family was a comfort to Mother, and I'm sure you continue to be.

This time, nothing will interfere. I will be there on April 16, and will tell her so as soon as we are back in touch. It sounds like she is doing well. Sunday draws near . . . Mother will have to call soon or risk having me get her answering machine.

Julie agreed. Mrs. Smith would have to decide what she was going to do. Julie just hoped she would be telling all. Finally, Ned's personality seemed to be coming through in his posts, and she liked what she saw. She especially liked the fact that he was sharing his thoughts about his mother's behavior. Only a good son would be concerned; she was glad that Ned seemed to be proving that he was one.

Chapter Three

Ned found himself looking forward to checking his email. He still had spam touting online pharmacies or "girls!girls!girls!", but his eyes quickly scanned the row of messages looking for the one from j_wong. Even Ellen, his secretary, had noticed a difference.

"Working at home for a couple of days seemed to do you good," she told him. "You look more relaxed."

Embarrassed, he mumbled something that might have been an agreement and busied himself with the memos and messages she handed him until she left the room. As soon as he was alone, he clicked open his email account.

Your mother continues doing well. She spent all of her free time yesterday working on the Hawaiian quilt pillow top the others helped her start. With

39

her stitching and piano playing, she claims not to have a moment to herself. And today, the residents started playing cards. Mrs. Akaka, your mom's new best friend, started them on it, but everyone has become very enthusiastic. Be assured, your mother makes this claim of not having any time to spare with a pleased smile. Yesterday I heard her say that she thought this must be something like having a group of sorority sisters, something she had not experienced during her college years.

Ned found himself grinning at the computer screen, even as he shook his head. She was playing cards? He didn't ever recall seeing his mother play cards. Except for go fish or hearts—with him when he was a child. What was she playing? Bridge seemed like the kind of game elderly women might play, but it took time to learn. Gin rummy perhaps. That was easy.

Reading her email on Friday morning, Julie frowned at the computer screen as she saw that Ned had picked up on her card-playing comment.

Have never seen mother play cards. Except for childhood games with me, of course. Somehow, I don't see senior citizens playing old maid or go fish—unless it's with their grandchildren.

Julie felt sure he'd smiled as he posted this. The thought of a full smile on that handsome visage caused a frisson of pleasure in her midsection that brought a smile to her lips. Followed by a rapid frown. Was she falling for a man who lived five thousand miles away? Because he was good looking and had a sense of humor?

Her smile faded as she returned to reading.

What do they play—gin rummy? Mother doesn't play bridge, and I know she'd need more than a day or two to learn it.

He wanted details. Julie's heart plummeted. Wait until he heard they were playing Texas hold'em. It was, after all, the latest rage. And just because they were old, didn't mean they didn't want to keep up with trends. She just hoped he wouldn't think the place was rife with card sharks trying to take advantage of the frail, elderly population.

Julie laughed at her own joke as she peeked out into the community room. The Hale Maika'i residents might be elderly; some of them were even frail. But none of them were weak in spirit or determination.

Six of the women, Claudia and the almost one-hundred year-old Mrs. Akaka among them, were sitting at one of the smaller tables, the cards spread out in typical poker fashion. They were all concentrating on the dealer as she laid out the next three cards. The flop, Julie had learned this was called. There was no laughing and chatting during this round. Julie had observed that they saved that for the time spent shuffling. While the play went on, they were serious. A fairly large heap of shells sat in the center of the table. Julie had to laugh when she first discovered that they had searched the craft supply closet looking for something to use for chips. What they'd settled on was a large bag of shells, already punctured and ready to string into leis. They did put everything back in the bag when they were done, and even returned the shells to the closet. But they carefully counted everyone's shell supply at the end of each session and Mrs. Akaka was keeping a careful tally. Bragging rights were everything at their age.

Julie returned to the computer to see what else Ned had written. She was tickled that he'd recently opened up more.

Your mention of cards reminds me of the games Mother and I played in my childhood days. We played go fish and hearts. I think she showed me how to play old maid, but I quickly decided that was too much of a "sissy" game for me. After all, a man couldn't be an old maid, right?

Julie smiled at his comment. Actually, she'd known at least one man who could easily have qualified as an old maid. Should she share that information with Ned? Would it make him smile?

I guess it's a good thing that Mother is busy and distracted while her leg heals. I have worried that she is becoming a recluse, although I know that your family tries to include her in your activities. I am appreciative of that BTW. Let me offer you and your family an official and sincere thank you for that consideration.

Julie frowned at the screen. He did have a tendency to be pompous. Still, he'd opened up a lot since that first email. And his thank you, pretentious as it was, showed that his heart was in the right place. By the time Mrs. Smith actually contacted him, he might sound like a normal person.

Biting back a smile, Julie began to type her reply.

Friday seemed to be Ned's day for surprises. Looking out his office window at noon, he'd been startled to see women sitting in the adjacent plaza sunning their bare arms. They were experiencing a spell of spring weather after the recent cold, with temperatures in the fifties and brilliant, sunny skies. But it had cooled again with the sun's retreat, and he found himself longing for the tropical heat of Hawaii. Just one more week. Meanwhile, he had his secret correspondence to peruse.

He was smiling even before he opened the email from Julie. Could the secrecy be part of the appeal of their little exchanges? More and more he wondered about Julie herself. Was she his age? Younger? He knew from her notes that she liked her job and was concerned about the happiness and well-being of all the people in the care center. It was a characteristic he'd not noticed in any woman he'd dated, and it made him wonder if only shallow women appealed to him.

No, of course not, he thought, though his smile began to fade. If that was the case, he wouldn't be so curious about Ms. Wong.

His smile morphed into a full-fledged frown.

Dear Ned,

I enjoyed hearing your reminiscences of early card games with your mom. But it isn't hearts or rummy that is taking up the residents' time these days. I'm afraid that Texas hold'em is the game of choice at the Hale Maika'i.

Texas hold'em!? Ned was stunned. His mother—his sweet, conservative, church-going mother—was playing Texas hold'em! How had that happened? How could the staff condone it? What happened to Julie's strong moral sense, the one that caused her to contact him in the first place?

He read further.

A few sessions on television and they were hooked. They might be old, but they like to be in on the latest fads. Mrs. Akaka, who turns one hundred later this month, says it makes her feel young to keep up with all the latest trends. And why not?

Why not? *Why not!?!* What about discouraging addictive behavior, and encouraging good moral conduct? What about gambling and losing money?

He frowned, running his hand over his face and closing his eyes for a moment. What about being a stuffed shirt? Boy, he needed that vacation more than he realized.

He turned his attention back to the computer screen.

For chips, they use some shells they found in the craft closet, supplies for stringing shell leis.

Ned drew his fingers through his hair, pushing the whole mess off his forehead. Among the things he ignored in April was a regular haircut. He'd have to have it done after he arrived in Hawaii or he'd look like an unkept bum.

I'm waiting for the day they begin to string up their winnings and wear them around their necks. To intimidate the others, you know.

He had to laugh.

Then he stopped, stunned by the sound of his own laughter. The first week in April, and he was laughing over an email message. In all the years he'd been doing taxes, he couldn't remember being so relaxed during the first week of April. He didn't want to believe that he was happy his mother had tripped over the dog and broken her leg, but he was certainly glad that Julie had defied her wishes and contacted him. He was getting more involved in his mother's life, and it felt good. At odd moments during the day, he found himself thinking about the residents of the Hale Maika'i, which was certainly better for his mental health than worrying over Mr. Fieldstone's tax deductions or Ms. Trumain's charitable contributions.

As he heated yet another frozen dinner in the microwave, he wondered what happened with Mr. Morimoto's quilt designs. Had Julie found a place for them in the local quilt shop? He'd gone so far as to Google Hawaiian quilt patterns to see what they were all about. His partner's mother was a quilter and he had a large quilt hanging on his office wall, right behind his desk. He claimed it gave the office a warm, homey feel that put clients at ease.

"I didn't make this up, Ned," Tyler told him. "They've done studies. They hang quilts in clinics and doctor's offices for the same reason. You should get one for your office."

Ned had gone so far as to look at the photos Tyler brought in of some other quilts his mother had available. But none of them appealed to Ned. The Hawaiian quilts he'd seen online though . . . those were something. He'd love a quilt like that in his office. He'd have to speak to his mother about it. If she was taking up the craft, perhaps she would make a wall hanging for him.

Julie's morning was more hectic than usual. Fridays were often busy as Julie handled arrangements for temporary residents who were heading home or permanent residents who spent weekends with family.

But that Friday morning, Mr. Jardine arrived. The curmudgeonly but popular old gentleman was well known around Malino, and his arrival had thrown the place into another upheaval. He would be spending a week in the rehab center while recovering from minor surgery. A life-long smoker, he was extremely put out when told he could not smoke in his room or in the larger common room, but would have to go outside to the garden. Though of course, they would prefer that he not smoke at all—which brought some strong language that upset a few of the more conservative patients.

So it wasn't until lunchtime that Julie finally sat at her desk and pulled up her email.

Her tight shoulders relaxed as she spotted Ned's address, almost hidden among the offers for cheap watches and inexpensive software. A tingling in her chest moved to her belly as she clicked on his name. And she didn't think it had anything to do with the quick bite of her tuna sandwich she'd had as she turned on the computer.

Aloha, *Julie.*
We had a beautiful sunny day here today. Nothing like your tropical heat I'm sure, but a lot of people were out enjoying the sun and warmth at lunch time.

He didn't say so, but Julie knew he wasn't one of those who spent some time outside enjoying the warm sun. She hoped Claudia was correct in thinking that he would rush to her side as soon as he heard about her injury. The man obviously needed a vacation. Still, the fact that he'd mentioned the sunshine meant he'd at least noticed it.

Julie popped the top on a can of orange-passion drink and took a long sip, then another bite of her sandwich. With the number of emails she still had to sort through, she could only justify lingering over Ned's correspondence if she ate her lunch at the same time.

Still, she couldn't resist indulging in a bit of fantasy—she and the luscious Ned sunning themselves on a local beach. The thought brought a smile to her lips and a delightful tingle to her tummy that quickly spread throughout her body. She felt warm all over, as though she really were sunbathing at Hapuna Beach.

Blinking away her daydreams, she returned to his note, slightly embarrassed by her fantasies. Not having a date for six months was no excuse for falling for a man she'd never met.

Mother playing Texas hold'em. It boggles the mind.

What do you think will happen when she returns home? Will she retreat into herself again? This new picture you've drawn for me is a good one, and I hope to encourage it.

Any news yet on whether she'll be home on Sunday?

A good question. Julie would have to check on that as soon as she finished with her lunch.

However, she still had half a sandwich left when Claudia herself appeared at her office door. With a guilty movement that she hoped her neighbor would not notice, Julie quickly closed the open email window on her computer. For good measure, she also adjusted the angle of the screen, away from her visitor's chair.

Claudia's crutches made heavy clumping noises on the hardwood floor as she entered Julie's office. Claudia had opted for the type of crutch that attached to the lower part of the arm and looked similar to a cane. She wore one on each wrist and declared them much easier on an old body that those "horrid things that go under your arm and cause great pain."

Julie hopped up, hovering beside her desk until Claudia was settled. She didn't want to offer unwanted aid, but she did want to be available if help was needed. Once Claudia lowered herself into the visitor's chair, Julie resumed her seat behind the desk, smiling her welcome.

"Hi, Mrs. Smith," she said, hoping she didn't appear as nervous and guilt-ridden as she felt. "It looks like you're managing those crutches like an old pro already."

Claudia took her time setting the two crutches beside her, propping them carefully against the arms of the chair. She seemed troubled and Julie wondered if she had come to plead the case for returning to her own home.

"I hope you aren't here to request that you go back home." Julie began, frowning slightly. "I can see how well you're walking now, but managing on your own without the free use of your hands is quite another matter. Why cooking alone . . ."

"Oh, I know that." Claudia fluttered one hand at her, not even apologizing for the interruption, a decidedly un-Claudialike action. "At first I thought I'd be able to manage on my own," Claudia admitted, "but now I can see that I wouldn't even be able to refill Ginger's water bowl." She sighed with real regret. "It's amazing to me how much I miss that dog," she said. "I've never had a dog before—or any kind of pet. But now I can't imagine *not* having one."

Julie nodded, putting on what she hoped was an encouraging expression.

"Actually," Claudia continued, "I came to ask your advice."

Julie waited while Mrs. Smith took a deep breath. She seemed to be thinking over whatever it was she wanted to say.

"You see, it's my son."

Suddenly, Julie found it difficult to take a breath. She stole a quick peek at her computer where the screensaver had kicked in.

Claudia didn't notice her discomfort. "He calls me every Sunday," she went on, "like clockwork. Right at noon, our time."

"That's nice," Julie murmured. Of course, she already knew this, had heard it from her neighbor any number of times as well as from Ned.

"He's very punctual. He's an accountant, you know."

"Yes, you've told me."

Claudia sighed. "Actually, I think he's rather a boring young man, but he's my son and I love him." She looked earnestly into Julie's eyes. "He *is* very handsome—looks just like his father," she added with a sigh of remembrance. "He wanted to get me a cell phone for Christmas last year, and I said no." She sighed again. "Now I'm sorry I didn't agree, even if I'm not sure I could ever learn how to use one."

"They really aren't that difficult, Mrs. Smith," Julie said. "I'd help you."

"Thank you," Claudia replied. "However, remember I told you not to tell him about my accident?"

"Ahh, yes." Julie swallowed hard. "I do remember." She wasn't lying, she told herself; she didn't say anything about whether or not she'd obeyed that request.

"Well, I never did call him myself. I meant to, but I've been so busy here with my new friends and all the activities. So now I'm concerned about Sunday." Her eyes met Julie's across the desk. She seemed to be trying to read something in Julie's face. "What do you think, Julie? Should I call him now, or wait until a minute before noon on Sunday?"

Julie gulped in air. This was great. She'd just tell her to call now.

But Julie apparently took too much time trying to get her guilt-ridden thoughts in order. Claudia began to speak again before she was able to say anything.

"It's hard for me to decide just what to do." She looked over at Julie, surprising her with the calculating expression in her eyes. "I don't suppose you'd come and pick me up on Sunday so I could go home long enough to take the call?"

Julie's eyes widened in surprise. "Mrs. Smith! I'm ashamed of you, plotting like that. You know you have to tell your son about this. I wasn't too happy with your decision to keep him in the dark earlier. But now you're asking me to help you deceive him. I just wouldn't feel right about that." Guilt consumed her; she was lying by omission to this sweet woman.

Claudia nodded. "I had a suspicion you might say that. Oh, well, I guess it will be all right. He's so busy at this time of year, he might not even take in what I say."

Julie was shocked now. "How can you say that! He's your son—your only relative. I'm sure he loves you and will be concerned for your welfare. You can have him call here and speak to Mrs. Fujita, or myself, or any of the other workers if it will help him feel more at ease." Guilt stabbed Julie, and the ache in her chest seemed real enough to be caused by a knife blade. Well, maybe a hat pin, one of those big old-fashioned ones.

Unaware of her companion's feelings of guilt, Claudia prattled on. "Thank you, dear, but I doubt that will be necessary. He is a good boy, it's just that he's so involved in his work, especially at this time of the year. He'll be distracted. It's not that he doesn't love me."

Julie lifted her hand, rubbing at the tense muscles at the back of her neck.

"Well then, I'll need your help," Claudia was saying.

"Certainly, what can I do?"

"I know you don't work on weekends, but I don't have Ned's phone numbers here with me. And I've been using the speed dial on the phone at the house, so

I don't know the number by heart. Could you run over to my house and pick up my address book tonight? Then, if you could bring it by tomorrow, maybe you could sit with me while I tell him. For moral support, you know."

Her expression was so wistful, Julie hadn't the heart to say no. "Of course," she said. Besides, it was a small thing, especially compared to what she'd already done.

"I don't mind getting the book for you, and you might like to have your phone numbers handy anyway in case there's anyone else you want to call," Julie said. "But I'll have to come by early in the morning. I promised Abby that I'd go shopping with her—for her wedding dress. Did I tell you she asked me to be her maid of honor?"

After exclaiming over this news, and with suitable congratulations, Claudia suggested, and Julie agreed, on seven the next morning.

"With the six-hour time difference, it will be a good time to call," Claudia added. "He'll probably be on a break, eating his lunch."

Chapter Four

Ned worked at home on Saturday morning, finally breaking for lunch just before one. He put a microwave dinner into the microwave and punched the timer. While he waited for his meal, he flipped open the laptop he'd brought into the kitchen. His fingers hovered over the touch pad; should he check email before he continued working?

With an impatient shake of his head, Ned bypassed the mailbox icon and opened a business file. He didn't know what had gotten into him lately. He'd never been obsessed by mail before.

The microwave chimed and he took his meal out, letting it sit on the table beside him for the five minutes called for in the directions. But seeing the small plate in front of him made him wonder what his mother was eating.

How was the food at the care center? Institutions were notorious for bad food. He hoped she was getting things she liked to eat, though he was aware his mother would eat whatever was put in front of her, just to be polite.

He realized that he knew nothing about what constituted local food in Hawaii. He was sure people didn't have *luaus* every day, and ground-roasted pig and fresh pineapple were the only things that came to mind when he thought of Hawaiian food.

On an impulse, he pulled up Google and typed in Hawaiian food. There were over seven million hits. The first site he opened turned out to be a list of Hawaiian food words. There were a lot of fish names on the list, as well as such strange items as *malasadas*, oxtail soup, *limu,* and *manapua. Manapua,* he discovered, was a type of Chinese roll filled with meat or beans, *limu* was the Hawaiian word for seaweed, and *malasadas* were Portuguese donuts, without holes. He wondered if Mother ate these things now. He liked fish, but the thought of eating seaweed didn't appeal.

He felt better when he found a newspaper survey about local food spots in the islands. Happily, steak houses and Italian restaurants were prominent, so he probably wouldn't have to try *limu* or *manapua* during his visit. *Malasadas,* though, sounded promising. He wouldn't mind trying those for breakfast one day.

A loud rumble from the direction of his midsection made him realize his lunch was cooling while he continued to surf online.

Slamming his laptop closed, Ned ripped the cellophane top off his meal and carried it into the other room. He turned on the television and started to eat. He'd watch the game. There was always a game on a Saturday afternoon.

But the television happened to be on the Travel Channel, and what he saw was not a basketball court filled with tall, sweating men, but swaying palm trees and serene blue waters. Then the scene changed and a dozen attractive and exotic young women swayed together in a *hula*. There was a special on about Hawaii. The entire world was conspiring against him.

The phone rang. Grateful for the distraction, Ned almost groaned aloud when he saw the 808 area code on his caller ID. So much for lunch. Unless Julie had abandoned mail for the phone, it looked like his mother was finally ready to let him in on her recent medical history.

Julie watched Claudia as she waited for her son to pick up. The granola bar she'd downed before leaving the house had become a hard lump in her belly. Her fingers fluttered in her lap, as jittery as a hummingbird's wings. Could she be nervous that Claudia might pass the phone to her? That she'd have to speak to Ned? It seemed unlikely, yet what other explanation was there for her clammy palms and rapidly beating heart?

Perhaps the churning in her belly had to do with the possibility that this phone call would mean the end of their correspondence. In a mere four days, she felt she'd gotten to know a lot about Ned, and she looked forward to his notes, to the opportunity to learn more about him. She enjoyed sharing her daily experiences with him, and was proud of the fact that she was help-ing him get reacquainted with his mother.

Julie was so taken up by her troublesome thoughts, she didn't even hear Claudia's conversation with her son. Until Claudia spoke her name and held the phone out.

At a loss, Julie stared blankly at Mrs. Smith.

"Go on, Julie. I told him about my broken leg. I just want you to assure him that I'm all right and happy here. And that he doesn't have to rush over."

Julie managed to wrap her fingers around the cool plastic, bringing it slowly to her ear. Why was she sud-denly so hesitant? She'd been anxious enough to email him, back when she didn't have permission. Yet now, with Mrs. Smith beside her, she was reluctant to speak to him.

"Hello?"

The voice carried to her ear, even though she still hadn't placed the receiver properly against it.

"Hello," he said again. "Anyone there?"

This time she heard him clearly. A baritone voice. His pronunciation was crisp, his vowels sharp—definitely a mainland voice. You couldn't tell a lot about someone from three words, but she liked his voice. It insinuated itself into her mind, flowed into her bloodstream, and warmed her from head to toe. The timbre and quality were such that it inspired trust; you could share private information with the owner of that voice, a good trait for someone in his business.

Julie cleared her throat before offering a tentative hello, worried that her voice might emerge as a squeaky soprano, relieved to hear her usual deeper tones.

For Mrs. Smith's sake, she tried to sound businesslike. Julie felt as though she and Ned were old friends, and she didn't want to let Claudia know that.

"This is Julie Wong."

"What? No *aloha?*"

Julie could hear the amusement in his voice and some of her nervousness fled.

"Of course. *Aloha.*"

Mrs. Smith leaned toward her, as though hoping to listen in, and Julie prayed Ned would be discrete.

"Your mother is doing very well here," she said.

"I'm glad to hear that. I am concerned of course. She says she's fine."

"Yes, she is." Julie swallowed, the beginning of a grin creeping onto her lips. Ned knew all this from her emails, but they'd have to go through the charade for Claudia's sake—on the off chance that she could hear what Ned was saying. "She's become very involved with the group activities here. She's made a lot of friends. Your mother is a wonderful addition to the Hale Maika'i. The other residents are going to miss her when she leaves."

"I'm glad to hear she's making friends."

Julie breathed a little easier. Ned must have recognized the possibility that his mother might overhear what was being said. He certainly knew about the new friends she'd made; she spent most of her emails talking about them.

"Perhaps she can continue to visit in the future."

"A wonderful idea." Julie smiled across her desk at Claudia. "He suggests you visit after you return home," she told her.

"That's a good idea," Claudia replied. "I thought of it myself."

"Did you hear that?" she asked Ned. He replied that he did.

"Feel free to call if you have any questions," Julie said, providing the Hale phone number and her extension before passing the phone back across the desk.

Claudia took it and spoke for a few minutes longer, nodding her head at whatever Ned was telling her. She smiled benignly at Julie after hanging up.

"Thank you so much for helping me with that, Julie. I didn't want to explain everything myself. It was wonderful having your support."

Surprised, Julie stood and moved around her desk. "You did a super job," she assured her, putting her hand on the older woman's shoulder. "I don't know why you were worried." Beneath her hand, she felt Claudia relax.

"He'll be coming on the sixteenth for a visit," Claudia said. "I told you he'd want to come right out, but I think hearing your assurances helped him decide it was okay to wait."

Not sure what to say to that, Julie nodded.

"He actually suggested a visit when we talked at Christmas time. But then he didn't mention it again and I thought he'd forgotten."

"Didn't you remind him?"

"Oh, no, I couldn't do that." Claudia shook her head.

"I wouldn't want to put him in a spot, in case he changed his mind. He always has so much work to do, and I wouldn't want to interfere with his business."

Julie wanted to tell Claudia to assert herself more, but she managed to hold onto her comment. Claudia had taken the initiative a few times recently and Julie didn't want to undermine her new confidence.

They were leaving Julie's office when Abby burst through the Hale entrance. She waved a greeting toward the people in the common room as she sauntered up to Julie.

"I was afraid you'd get pulled into doing more work, so I decided to pick you up. I don't want to be late starting out."

She turned toward Claudia. "Hello Mrs. Smith. We're going shopping for wedding dresses. Did Julie tell you she's going to be my maid of honor?"

After that, they had to explain the shopping trip to everyone in the common room. Finally the women smiled, shooing them off. But not until extracting a promise from Julie to tell them all about it on Monday.

"Bring photos," Mrs. Akaka called after them.

The young women laughed, Abby looking back over her shoulder, her grin a mile wide. "My new cell phone takes pictures."

"So, tell me all about the phone call to Ned," Abby said, once they were settled in her little blue truck. "Did you talk to him?"

Julie didn't answer immediately. There hadn't been enough time for her to work out her reaction. How could she tell Abby that she was half in love with a man she'd never met? A man who looked terrific in a photo and sounded even better on the phone?

"Come on, girl. Yes? No?" Abby urged.

"Yes, I did."

"Great," Abby said. "Tell me all about it. What did he sound like? Did you tell Mrs. Smith that you two have been in touch?"

"Oh, no." Julie's startled reply was instantaneous. "I don't think either of us will tell her—since she asked me not to."

Julie reached over to pick up a bridal magazine that lay on the seat between them. A bit of torn paper marked a page. "Is this the dress you found—the one that's not a traditional frou-frou dress?"

At Abby's nod, she flipped the magazine open and admired the elegant dress pictured. Not an unaffordable Vera Wang, but obviously influenced by her style. "I hope this means I won't have to have one. A frou-frou dress I mean."

"Of course not," Abby said. "I don't like frou-frou. And you're avoiding my question about Ned," Abby reminded her.

Julie had hoped she wouldn't notice.

"So what did he sound like?" Abby asked, impatient to hear Julie's answer. "Sexy voice?"

For a moment, Julie looked back on her brief phone

conversation. She'd found Ned's voice appealing. The sound of it had made her all warm and fuzzy.

"Ned has a nice voice," Julie finally said.

"Nice voice. Oh, come on," Abby said, obviously disappointed. "You can do better than that."

"Can you believe I was nervous about talking to him?" she finally admitted. "And after all these days of emailing back and forth. I don't know what got into me. My stomach was a mess."

Abby's voice was softly careful. "It's been a long time since Lenny left, and you haven't been dating at all. Of course you got nervous thinking about talking to a guy you describe as 'gorgeous'."

"I'm a busy person," Julie countered. "I don't need to be dating to be a fulfilled woman."

"Good grief, you've been watching too much Oprah."

But Julie didn't even smile. "Actually, you were saying the same kind of thing not too long ago. For most of the past year in fact."

Abby had come back to Malino after breaking up with a long-time boyfriend and losing her job at a trendy Hollywood salon. The decision had been a happy one for both Julie and for Malino. Abby hadn't actually dated in the past year, claiming she'd sworn off men, but she'd become friends with a fire fighter—who had recently become her fiancé.

Abby had the grace to agree. Julie thought she even spotted some extra color in her cheeks. "I guess. Sometimes love can creep up on you," she said.

Julie frowned. "He's coming for a visit."

"Really?" Abby braked as a car pulled onto the highway from a side road. Once she had regained cruising speed, she went on. "That's great. When?"

"April sixteenth."

"I should have known." Abby chuckled, and Julie joined in. "You're sure to meet him."

Julie tried not to let on, but the thought of meeting Ned set a colony of butterflies loose in her stomach. Such a good-looking man, with such a soothing voice— like hot tea on a cool morning. And she felt sure he had a sense of humor eager to escape. She could tell that much from his photograph, and there had been more clues in his email.

"I'm sure Mom and Dad will have them over for dinner," Julie said. "You and Kevin can come too; he should meet some guys his age."

"I hadn't thought of that, but you're right. How old is he?"

"Early thirties. Do you think that's too old?" She stopped short of adding "for me?"

But Abby caught it anyway. "The man is a good age. In fact, he'll be bored to death if he has to spend all his time here with his mother. Especially since she has limited mobility right now. I realize he's coming to see her, but he can't be with her twenty-four, seven. Maybe Kevin can take him fishing or diving or something. What does he like to do?"

"I don't know."

Julie wanted to wail at Abby that she didn't know anything about Ned. Not that she should. It just bothered her a lot that she was so ignorant about him when she was half in love with him.

"I keep trying to tell you, I hardly know the man. We've only been in touch for a week and our emails are mostly about his mother." Which was why she was so concerned about her reaction this morning. Plain and simple, her body's response to a veritable stranger was completely uncalled for. But how did her mind relay that eminently sensible information to her completely impractical nervous system?

While Abby and Julie drove into Hilo, at the Hale Maika'i Claudia and Mabel were huddled together at one end of a long sofa. If Julie had seen them, it would have brought to mind Mrs. Smith's sweet comment about college days and sorority sisters. The two women were discussing men, too, just like college women so often do—but it wasn't because they were interested in dates for themselves. And while Julie might have been surprised to hear them discussing men as dating material for themselves, she would have been horrified to discover they were talking about possible dates for *her*.

"Julie is such a nice girl," Mabel was saying. "It's a shame she doesn't have a boyfriend. That fiancé of hers wasn't much of a catch and I'm sure she's better off without him, but she's not even dating after all this time. She must have really been hurt."

Claudia nodded. "Her aunt never liked him either. And Valerie, her mother you know," she added, in case Mabel wasn't on a first name basis with Julie's parents, "was always quiet when his name came up. I suspect she didn't want to say anything that wasn't nice. I never met him myself."

All the residents knew the story. Gossip about the staff was a popular leisure-time activity at the Hale. They called it their real-life soap opera and spent hours discussing the lives of the various employees. Julie's love life was a favorite topic because everyone liked her and wanted to see her happy. So it was inevitable that the others in the room would hear Julie's name and get involved.

"He came here a few times," Eleanor Milho said. "Wasn't very friendly. I don't think he liked old people."

"He wasn't a bad fellow," Fred Jardine said. Since he was a retired police detective with lots of experience regarding bad guys, the others reluctantly accepted his opinion. "Probably just afraid to think he'd be old himself one day."

"Well, Las Vegas is welcome to him, I say." The others agreed with Mabel.

"He did ask Julie to join him there," Claudia said.

"You always want to see the best in everyone," Mabel said, patting Claudia on the arm.

"Well, you can't fault a man for going where he can get a good job."

Eleanor and several others nodded. Most of them had at least one relative who'd recently moved to Nevada. The Las Vegas area had one of the largest Hawaiian populations on the mainland.

"Well, he wasn't a nice man—no matter what you

say, Fred," Mabel stated. She figured her ninety-nine-plus years entitled her to speak her mind. "If he loved Julie, he should have realized that she would never leave Malino," she said with a firm nod, setting her gray curls to bobbing.

"He broke her heart," Eleanor said, her voice dripping romantic tragedy.

But Claudia didn't agree. "I don't think she was as heartbroken as she expected to be. Her Aunty Claudia even thought she was relieved when it was definitely over." She lowered her voice, though it was unclear why. If she was trying to keep her words to her immediate neighbor, she failed miserably, as everyone in the room heard. "Claudia thought that Lenny was *gambling* over there, and trying to keep it from Julie."

"No!" Although Eleanor had claimed not to like Lenny, she seemed suitably shocked to hear this.

"Wouldn't be surprised," Fred commented. "Jobs aren't the only draw. I used to enjoy going to Vegas myself. Played a mean hand of blackjack," he said with satisfaction.

But Mabel wasn't interested in hearing about his gambling jaunts. She turned back to Claudia.

"So what's that son of yours like? You say he's coming to visit next weekend? Would he be good for our Julie?"

Five pairs of expectant eyes turned toward Claudia. She realized that a mere week ago, she would have been horrified by this conversation—discussing such personal things with all these other people. Now, however, she'd discovered the joys of friendship and regretted she hadn't learned it many years ago. But then she'd had such a close relationship with her pen pal Claudia, maybe having that one special alliance made up for the lack of any others. And perhaps it was the close living that brought about this kind of camaraderie.

"Well, Ned is *very* handsome," she said with a smile. "He looks just like his father did at that age. Unfortunately, I've always thought Ned was a bit boring," she confided. "But he's a good son and he works hard. I think he'd make someone an excellent husband."

"Well, I don't know," Mabel said. "Julie doesn't need a boring husband. She's a sweet, fun-loving person. She should have someone who'll do things with her."

"Oh, Ned does things. At least he used to before he got to working all the time." Claudia pursed her lips as she thought this over and realized it was true. He'd been an active and social young man until he took an internship during his college years. "I don't think that office is good for him. He works too hard."

"Some people love their work, so it's all they need." Mr. Morimoto's quiet words let them know just how he'd felt about his own career.

"That's true," Fred agreed. "But it's good to be well-rounded. You know what they say about all work and no play. I loved being a cop but I also liked hunting and fishing with friends. And a weekly game of poker."

Mabel fidgeted impatiently while others told of their hobbies. As soon as possible, she returned to the subject of Ned.

"What kinds of things did he do?" Mabel asked Claudia. "Before he started working all the time?"

"Oh, he played all the sports the young boys do. Baseball was his favorite, but he played football and soccer and basketball too. And he loved to swim. He'd be at the pool all summer long. He became a lifeguard in high school, and he went camping with the Scouts. He and his dad would go on fishing trips. He was always interested in boats. I remember making him a sailboat quilt when he was just a little guy, and he just loved it."

"Maybe you can get him to move here," Eleanor suggested. "There are a lot of water sports, so he might like it."

"He could have a boat here," Fred mentioned. "Maybe he'd like to join a canoe club. That's a great activity."

"It would be nice to have him nearby," Mabel said. "You're not getting any younger. You should be able to see him, and get to spend some time with the grand-children."

"He has to get married to have grandchildren," Claudia said.

"We should figure out how to get them together," Mabel suggested. "What do you think, Claudia?"

"Well, she will be right next door," Claudia reminded her. "And I'm sure Valerie will invite us for dinner. They're very kind that way."

"That's okay," Mabel agreed. "But we need something that puts them together—just the two of them. Who's going to pick him up at the airport?"

"I hadn't thought about it." Claudia frowned. "He'll probably rent a car."

"No, no," Mabel said, her eyes glittering with delight in planning this little coup. "You have a car, don't you?"

Claudia nodded.

"Tell him he can use your car while he's here. To save the expense, you know. You won't be going out much until that cast comes off anyway. And then you can ask Julie to pick him up."

"Oh, that's good." Claudia's laugh was close to a giggle. This matchmaking with her friends was fun! "Ned will appreciate the fact that I want to help him save money. And I'll bet Julie will be glad to help out."

"Then that will work." Mabel grinned, showing off a gold eye tooth. "Maybe she can show him around a bit too."

"But she'll have to work," Claudia reminded her.

"She doesn't work *all* the time. There are the evenings, and weekends."

The women's eyes glowed as they discussed the possibilities.

Before bedtime that evening, Julie opened her email as usual. She felt a pang in her chest as she clicked on the mailbox icon. She'd miss the notes from Ned. She might have made fun of his initial stilted style, but even then she'd enjoyed reading his messages and plotting how she might get a reaction from him.

As she scanned the subject lines, deleting the offers

of cheap pharmaceuticals and penny stocks, she was pleasantly surprised to find something from Ned.smith. The subject line read merely *Saturday*.

Smiling widely, Julie double-clicked on the message— a surprisingly long note from Ned, which added to her feeling of joy.

Aloha, *Julie. It was nice to talk to you. You have a very interesting voice.*

Julie stopped reading as her smile faded. What an odd thing to say. "A very interesting voice?" What on earth could he mean by that? Was "interesting" good or bad?

As I cleaned out my email folder this evening, I realized that I would miss your cheerful posts, so I was determined to send a note. This desire to keep up a correspondence that is unrelated to business is something new for me, especially so close to April 15. I credit your delightful stories of the Hale residents for making me feel more relaxed than I have ever been at this time of year. I've found myself looking forward to your messages. However, if I am to presume on you to continue writing, I feel I must contribute as well.

A wave of pleasure swept through Julie. This was a different Ned, a more casual one—despite his rather stilted language. She liked this new side of him, more than she cared to admit. And he'd called her stories delightful.

For the first time in years, I find my mind wandering from business matters in early April. I've looked up Hawaiian quilts so that I could see what Mother might be learning and how they differed from what might be called a typical quilt. I discovered that Hawaiian quilts are beautiful, and I hope Mother continues her interest. I'd love a small quilt for my office wall.

I don't suppose you'd care to suggest it.

Julie found her grin widening. She liked this new Ned.

While I heated a microwave meal for today's lunch, I found myself Googling Hawaiian food. There were a lot of foods listed that I am not familiar with, but I noticed that a local newspaper survey of restaurants included Italian and Chinese among the favorites. Perhaps you and I can have dinner together one night during my visit, as a thank you for the care you've shown mother. Italian is a personal favorite; is there a local spot you can recommend?

Julie swallowed heavily at the casual invitation. How unexpected. And how exciting. Her stomach did a little flip as she thought of having an actual date with Ned. Movie-star handsome Ned with the smile just itching to explode into laughs.

Suddenly, the room felt incredibly warm. She checked to be sure the window was open and saw the curtain flutter with the mountain breeze.

Still, she gave a wry smile at how little he knew Malino. They had two eating places in their tiny town, a Japanese lunch shop that closed by two each afternoon, and a café locally referred to as "the seafood place"— because the original tenant had been a seafood restaurant. There had been several other restaurants with various specialties occupying the space since, but locals continued to call it "the seafood place." Still, he'd invited her out to dinner. Abby would definitely call that a date;—and probably remind her that the seafood place served spaghetti.

Julie smiled, feeling a welcome warmth encircle her heart and spread outward through her body. She'd call that a date too.

Chapter Five

Mondays were always hectic, but this one was even worse than usual. When Julie finally had a moment alone in her office, she went instantly to her email folder. She and Ned had exchanged short notes on Sunday and she could already feel herself relaxing at the thought of telling him about her hectic morning.

A glimmer of a smile touched her lips as she formed sentences in her head, waiting for the proper windows to open. She'd had a dreadful morning, but just the thought of sharing the details with Ned was lifting her mood. In their latest messages, they'd talked about favorite foods, discovering that pizza with pepperoni and green peppers was a shared favorite as well as sweet and sour chicken, and shrimp—however it was fixed. Reading his further comments about food, and a tentative start to a discussion of music, released a bit more of the morning's stress.

73

By the time she recounted her version of the morning, she felt one hundred percent better. The afternoon was sure to improve. She was still working on plans for Mrs. Akaka's hundredth birthday party, and she'd just heard from the mayor's office that he would be stopping by. She couldn't help smiling as she wondered whether the guest of honor would be honored, or just look upon it as her due.

Ned had taken to checking his email just before leaving for the day. With the time difference between Syracuse and Malino, that seemed to be the best time to find mail from Julie. On Monday evening, he was chuckling over Julie's long post about her morning when his secretary popped in to tell him she was leaving. She seemed surprised to see him smiling at the computer monitor.

"It's nice to see you taking a break," she told him. "Did someone forward you a joke?"

"Ah, no." Ned found himself strangely embarrassed. A motherly woman with snow-white hair and a generous figure, Ellen was the same age as Claudia and often used the age difference to mother him. Now he felt a need to explain his levity. "It's a note from my mother's neighbor. She's been keeping me apprised of her condition."

Ellen knew all about his mother's accident and had already purchased his plane tickets for the following weekend.

"I'm glad you're going to visit her. You should have gone long before this."

Some of his friends would be horrified to be spoken to by a secretary in such a manner, but Ned accepted her chiding in the spirit she intended. Ellen was an old family friend who'd needed a job just at the time he was starting up his office. Their working relationship was excellent, and he loved her like a favorite aunt.

"If it happens again, you just make me some reservations and hand me the ticket."

"You think I won't?" She laughed, and Ned joined in. "Anyway, I just wanted to let you know I'll be going now . . ."

Ned watched fondly as she left his office, then turned his attention back to Julie's latest email.

Dear Ned,

I'm so glad you want to continue the correspondence. It seems natural to tell you about the dreadful day I'm having. Once I tell you about it, I hope I'll be able to dismiss it from my mind and continue into the afternoon with a better attitude.

I guess it's just been a classic Monday. Before I could even get to my office this morning, Mr. Morimoto and his daughter, Annie, caught me. This is a good thing, it was just frustrating to be caught with my arms filled and unable to excuse myself without seeming rude. Annie has Mondays off and usually comes over to spend time with her father. She'd been concerned about him, and had talked to the staff doctors because she feared he was depressed. Poor man so missed working in his garden, but the doctors told him he could no longer work outdoors. And tending a few indoor plants she got for him just doesn't seem to be the same. But now that he has his artwork, he is so much better. She was very complimentary, actually, thanking me for getting him started, and assuring me that she would bring him more supplies in the future. They even presented me with a lovely watercolor he did of some plumerias from the back garden. I'm going to have it framed to hang in my office.

I'd no sooner gotten into my office and dropped everything on my desk—I've decided I carry way too many things in every morning, and will have to do something about that. My arms were tired (!!) after standing there talking to them for so long.

But anyway, I hadn't even had time to sit down and the phone rang. It was the son of one of the residents, calling to complain because he heard about the poker games. Even my assurances that no money changed hands weren't enough for this person—who doesn't even live in town BTW. He was calling from the mainland. Went on and on about the evils of gambling. Can you really call it gambling if you're playing for a handful of shells—and shells already punctured for stringing at that, so how much value can they have. Sheesh!

When I finally got off the phone, I had to referee a petty argument between two of the women. One woman accused the other of stealing her talcum powder, of all things. It turned out they each had a box of the exact same stuff. But it took almost an hour to hear both sides of the story and get everything worked out.

And, I'm supposed to be organizing Mrs. Akaka's 100 birthday celebration. We had a lovely party for her last year, so this year's will have to be even better. She's a wonderful woman, very spry for her age. I want to do something special. It takes so much longer than I expect to arrange these things. But happily, I did hear from the mayor's office this morning, and he's going to stop by to wish her a happy birthday. That will garner some nice publicity—he's sure to bring a photographer, maybe even a television reporter—and she'll be tickled.

I'm sorry to impose upon you, venting this way, but I feel so much better now. I'm going to eat my lunch—a very nice ham and cheese sandwich on wheat bread—and then I'll be able to face the afternoon with a cheerful face. I'll take up your discussion of music tomorrow if you don't mind. Writing to you is better than seeing a psychologist. Cheaper too.

Aloha, *Julie*

While taking a break earlier in the day, Ned had done a Google search for the Hale Maika'i and discovered a Web site. With photos. So he was able to picture Julie now, who he'd found smiling at the camera in a photo from last year's birthday bash for Mrs. Akaka.

He'd been taken by her round, friendly face, her expression open and with a smile sweeter than Splenda. He could easily imagine her standing there with her arms loaded down with books, craft supplies, her purse, and her lunch, waiting patiently for Mr. Morimoto and his daughter to have their say. It was harder to imagine her frustrated over her busy morning acting as complaint department and referee. Proud to think he'd helped her out, even in such a passive manner, he clicked on REPLY.

Julie didn't get back to the computer until after she got home that night. Her afternoon had not been better than the morning. In fact, things had gotten steadily worse.

For the first time since her breakup with Lenny, she missed him. Or maybe it wasn't him specifically she missed, just the *idea* of a steady boyfriend. Tonight, she would have enjoyed a relaxing evening, perhaps a quiet dinner for two, or taking in a silly movie. She definitely would have appreciated a sympathetic chest to lay her head on and a comforting arm around her shoulders.

Instead, she ate with her parents. And while they did listen compassionately to her recounting of her day— something Lenny probably would not have done— parents just weren't the same. She longed for that one someone special who would put his arm around her and hold her close to comfort her.

As soon as she got to her room, she booted up the computer. A few games of spider solitaire would settle her down. But once the computer was on, she couldn't resist peeking into her email folder. Finding a response from Ned to her earlier post did more to elevate her mood than the long talk with her parents.

Cringing over the email she'd sent off at lunchtime, which now seemed like a whiny rant, she opened this latest offering. Scanning it quickly, she smiled, then settled down for a slower read.

Dear Julie,

I am glad that the emails continue. It was obvious to me that today's message was indeed necessary—for your peace of mind. I did not feel imposed upon. In fact, I actually chuckled over your description of the group of events that sabotaged your morning. My secretary, who is an old family friend and often seems to think she is my mother BTW, actually complimented me for taking a break from business matters. She asked if someone had forwarded a joke.

I hope your afternoon improved and that you were able to plan a wonderful party for Mrs. Akaka. And perhaps you should arrange a shopping trip so that you can acquire a large briefcase? I carry a rather large one myself, as I do a lot of work at my home office. I'm not sure I understand just what it is you take back and forth, but you should find a convenient way to manage it. Perhaps one of those crates with the wheels and pull-up handles that are popular right now. I see people dragging them in and out of the building filled with boxes and file folders.

I will look forward to hearing about your taste in music. I hope you enjoyed your lunch. Personally, I prefer ham and cheese on rye. With mustard, of course, and lettuce and tomato.

Sincerely, Ned

Julie grinned, tickled by the juxtaposition of intimate confidences and formal language.

Consultations and phone calls kept Ned busy through lunchtime on Tuesday. When she came back from her own lunch, Ellen brought him a sandwich and urged him to take a break.

"You need a moment to relax," she told him. "I'll monitor your calls for the next fifteen minutes."

Smart woman that she was, she knew he wouldn't allow himself more than that. Still, it was plenty of time to check his email. And there, halfway down the list of new messages, was the one from j_wong.

Dear Ned,

Thank you so much for responding to my earlier rant in such a sane manner. I'm afraid my afternoon did not improve. In fact, things just got worse. Right after lunch, Mrs. Milho complained of chest pains that grew bad enough to require a call to 9-1-1. The excitement caused by her possi-

ble heart attack, plus the arrival of the fire truck and paramedics created more excitement, triggering an attack of Mr. Morimoto's emphysema. Luckily, Mr. Morimoto's breathing was stabilized without requiring a trip to the hospital. And we eventually learned that Mrs. Milho did not have a heart attack, just an attack of angina. So the day did end well. Tomorrow has to be better, don't you think?

Your light-hearted note has helped me immensely. As has dinner with my parents, who listened sympathetically while I talked and talked—right after I told them that I didn't want to talk about my awful day. Our emails have become such an important part of my day, I'm glad you don't want to drop them completely.

BTW your mother was an island of sanity during the whole mess this afternoon. She helped calm Mrs. Kahea, who was quite agitated by all the unusual activity. Mrs. Kahea, who suffers from early Alzheimer's, is easily rattled by any change in the routine, and your mother was just wonderful with her. She took her outside to sit in the garden, and they made leis together—to have for welcoming Mrs. Milho back later, she told her. It was a lovely thing to do, and such a help for the staff members who were so busy with two emergencies. With a mother like that, I'm not surprised that you are so good with my little tirades. You apparently learned from an expert.

Once again, Ned found a comment of Julie's about his mother catching him by surprise. He realized that he'd been so little in her life these past few years that he didn't know how she might handle an emergency.

Then, in another precipitate action totally unlike his usual careful self, he picked up the phone and called the Hale Maika'i. He did have the presence of mind to check the clock and do the figuring that assured him Julie should be at her desk.

But she wasn't.

In Malino, Julie was running late. She'd just arrived at work when she heard her phone ring. Rushing in to answer it, her hello sounded breathless and completely unprofessional. Too late, she thought she should have allowed it to go to voice mail. Until she realized who was on the other end.

"Ned?"

"Is today any better?"

Julie experienced a pleasant surge of surprise. Ned. Calling her to see how her day was going after the disaster of Monday!

"Did you want to speak to your mother?" she asked, tamping down the pleasure that surged through her. She might be presuming too much. Perhaps he was concerned for his mother after reading about yesterday's problems. "She's okay."

"No, I called to talk to you."

For a moment, Julie found herself speechless, but she did recognize the little thrill that passed through her.

Happiness. She was happy to hear from him. Happy he cared. And afraid to analyze her feelings any further.

"I only have a few minutes, but I just read the email you sent last night," Ned said, "and felt you could use some good wishes. I hope this morning will proceed in better fashion."

Julie was touched, even as she suppressed a giggle at his language. So it wasn't only on paper that he talked that way.

"As you probably realize, it's too early in the day to know," she replied, "but I have my fingers crossed. There can always be an emergency situation when you're working with senior citizens, but yesterday was the worse day we've had since I've been here."

"Statistics are against it happening again today."

Julie smiled. Leave it to an accountant to come up with that.

"What about things happening in threes?" she asked.

"Just a superstition. Besides, I have a feeling you are up to meeting any challenge."

His voice softened, turning to warm molasses. The tingle it sent through her heated her from head to heels.

Julie could hear voices at his end. A client must have entered his office.

"I'm afraid I have to go. I hope you have a quiet, peaceful day."

He hung up before she could wish him the same.

The warm glow caused by Ned's considerate phone call stayed with Julie for the rest of the day. And while her day wasn't exactly quiet, it was peaceful. Mrs. Milho was welcomed back with the leis made the day before, which had been carefully preserved in damp paper towels in the refrigerator.

That pleasant glow lingered as she walked to exercise class with Abby after work. Although it had rained that morning, the late afternoon was sunny and clear. Both women breathed in deeply, enjoying the agreeable scents of damp grass and soil, ocean brine and tropical flowers. The perfume of Malino.

"So, what do you hear from Ned?" Abby asked.

Julie hoped Abby didn't see the blush she felt tint her cheeks. "He called this morning." Before Abby could tease her about it, she went on. "I wrote him this rambling email about the horrid day I had yesterday," she explained. "And he was terrific. Sent me a note saying he hoped my day got better. Then when he got the second message about how much worse the day got . . ." Her grin was so wide, she thought all her teeth must be showing. She probably looked like a fool. "He wanted to wish me a quiet and peaceful day."

Abby grinned too. "Sounds like you're enjoying this."

Julie couldn't help but notice the amusement in Abby's voice.

"Isn't it funny how Mrs. Smith got to Malino because of writing to your aunt, and now you're meeting her son the same way? Sort of."

Julie had to admit that yes, it was an odd coincidence.

"I am enjoying this, but don't read too much into it," she warned. "He still lives far away. Where it snows," she added for good measure. Abby knew how much she disliked cold weather.

As Julie and Abby finished their exercise session, the residents of the Hale Maika'i finished up their dinner. Claudia and Mabel joined the others in the common room, but sat to one side.

"I've had the best idea," Mabel began, her voice filled with mischievous glee.

Claudia scooted her chair closer. The large television was tuned to "Wheel of Fortune," and the others were caught up in solving the puzzle, a large one with half the letters showing. "What is it?" she asked.

"I have a niece who entertains at the big *luau* they have twice a week at that big resort, the Anuenue. I was just thinking . . . that would be just the thing for your son to attend while he's here. Give him a nice taste of the islands, yeah?"

Claudia's eyes sparkled. She could already see the possibilities. "Mabel, that's a wonderful idea. A *luau* could be a very romantic setting, couldn't it?"

Mabel's answer was her characteristic, cacklelike chuckle. "Especially at the Anuenue. Have you ever been there?"

At Claudia's negative response, Mabel went on. "It's a beautiful place. The *luau* is held on this huge lawn, under the palm trees. The beach is rocky, but it still looks real good at night, and they won't be swimming anyway. It's very romantic with the torches lit and the wind blowing through the palm fronds, and the sound of the surf."

Claudia grinned. "I've always thought the sound of the wind in the palm trees is very romantic. Almost as nice as the waves breaking on the beach. And there they have both." She sighed, happy just thinking of the possibilities. "Torches and moonlight. It has potential."

"It would be perfect if there was a big bright moon that night."

Claudia's smile faded. "But how will we get Julie there?"

Mabel dismissed this concern with a flick of her wrist. "Julie is always eager to help out. All you have to do is say how you want Ned to have this wonderful island experience, but you don't feel up to spending the entire evening outside for the *luau* and entertainment. The lawn is uneven, the crowd might jostle your cast . . . you'll think of something."

Claudia nodded. "You're right. That would be just the thing to say to Julie. As soon as I ask if she might possibly help out, she'll offer to go." Claudia smiled happily. "Can your niece get the tickets for me?"

"I'll go call her right now." Mabel pulled her walker closer, raised herself off the sofa, and moved quickly from the room.

The brief phone calls became a daily routine. Ned would take a few minutes off at two o'clock every day. Five thousand miles away (give or take a few hundred) Julie would be at her desk by eight o'clock, ready to grab the phone at its first ring. They supplemented these brief conversations with longer emails.

Julie grabbed up the phone as soon as it rang on Wednesday morning. "Hey, good morning."

A low chuckle floated across miles and miles of wires and cables, perhaps even bouncing off a satellite or two. "The phone at your end didn't even ring," Ned informed her.

"Yes, it did. That's how I knew to pick it up." She couldn't kill the smile that brightened her face and her voice. "If you're trying to imply that I was just sitting here waiting for your call . . ." She paused, debating whether she should admit it. Oh, why not? "Well, you'd be right."

He could hear the smile and reciprocated with a grin of his own. "You realize these five minute calls are saving my sanity."

"So you've told me," she said.

Her admittance brought a moment of silence that left them both feeling warm and comfortable.

"So . . ." Julie finally said. "Tell me what you like to do. I thought I could introduce you to my friend Abby's fiancé. He's a firefighter, so he has days off during the week. Abby says he could take you fishing or diving or something, but I didn't know what you'd enjoy."

"I've always loved boats," he began. "Almost any type of water sport. I don't get much chance to do that here . . ."

"I remember you mentioning how you loved boats when you told me about the quilt your mom made for you."

"Yeah. Hearing about Mother's new pursuits have

had me revisiting my childhood. And I've discovered that I had a great childhood. I'd never thought about it before, but it's a good thing to know about yourself."

Before Julie had time to reply, their five minutes were up and Ned was called away. So Julie booted up the computer and followed up with an email.

So, I'm happy to hear you had a great childhood. So did I. I guess that means we're two happy, well-adjusted adults.

I hope you can take a few minutes to think about activities you might be interested in—for while you're here, I mean. You mentioned boats. So I'm assuming water sports. There are a lot. Not sure how much your mom will be able to do with you in that area. Will you want to spend all your time with her? But, what am I thinking?! I can hear her now . . . "You go on and do some fun things. I don't want to be a bother and keep you from having fun." So, FYI . . .

There are beautiful beaches near here, but not in Malino itself. We have a shorefront park but the beach is rocky and the undertow can be dangerous. But Hapuna Beach is close and it's like a postcard. Over half a mile of white sand beach, shallow water that deepens farther out. Great for swimming, snorkeling, bodysurfing, windsurfing. You can do board surfing at 'Anaeho'omalu Beach which is just a little further.

Then there's boating of various kinds . . . Atlantis

*submarine and glass bottomed boats if you go down
to Kona. You could do those with your mom. There's
also scuba and snuba. I already mentioned surfing
and wind-surfing, and there's also kayaking, outrigger canoe paddling, parasailing, deep sea fishing,
spear fishing . . .*

*As I said, the list goes on and on. Think about it.
I can't wait to see you in your beach togs. Bet
you'll look terrific in a tan!*

Reading Julie's note that evening, Ned found himself
wishing it was already Friday. Her flirty comment about
him in a tan made him more anxious than ever to meet
her in person. Not only that, he wanted to do everything
mentioned in her note, even though he knew there
would scarcely be time during a two week visit. Not
if he planned to spend quality time with his mother
as well.

"I'd enjoy deep sea fishing," he told Julie during
their phone conversation the next day. "I've always
wanted to try it. My father and I used to go on fishing
trips in the Finger Lakes."

As things grew more and more hectic, Ned found
these short calls to Hawaii almost a necessity. If the
feeling induced by his brief conversations with Julie
could be packaged as a stress reliever, he'd be a mil-
lionaire. He loved the sound of her voice. It intrigued
him that it didn't match the petite woman he saw pictured on the Web site. That woman should have a high,
girlish voice, not the low, sexy contralto that he heard

each afternoon. The one now saying, "The Finger Lakes? What an odd name."

He liked the way she accented her words, something he'd heard in the local actors employed in television shows filmed in Hawaii. It was very different from what you heard in Syracuse, and he found it charming.

He had to shake himself mentally to get his mind back on track and reply to her comment on the Finger Lakes.

"Well, they're long and narrow . . ."

". . . and look like fingers," she finished with him. They both laughed.

"On a map, they look like fingers," Ned said. "We also did a few fishing trips on Lake Ontario. Caught a twenty-five pound salmon one time, which was pretty exciting for a sixteen-year-old. But I guess that would be nothing compared to ocean fish."

"You're right. Marlin are easily into the hundreds of pounds. I'll talk to Kevin about it. He can probably arrange something. You two could go together . . . What about parasailing?" Julie asked. "Have you ever tried it? Where you're towed behind a boat held aloft by a parachute? It's a very touristy thing to do . . ."

"But I'll be a tourist, don't forget."

"Right." Julie didn't know why she couldn't seem to remember that. Maybe because he was Claudia's son and Claudia had become so much a part of the Wongs' life. "Anyway, I thought you might like that. There are several companies in Kona that do it. I could ask around for a recommendation on which one is best."

"Right. Have to go."

Julie could hear other voices at his end and she almost missed his final comment.

"I can't wait to see you in your bikini."

"Julie, I wonder if you could do me a favor." Claudia smiled sweetly at Julie . . .

"Of course." Julie had been turning to leave the common room when Claudia spoke, and she halted to hear what the older woman would say. It was quitting time, but it was so rare for Mrs. Smith to ask for favors, Julie was curious. Even if it made her late for Abby's aerobics class. "What can I do for you?"

"Well, Ned is coming in on Saturday, you know."

"Yes, I remember." Julie was looking forward to it too, even as she tried to remind herself that she was only interested because it meant so much to Mrs. Smith. She'd come to like Ned—perhaps too much—through their correspondence and wondered if Ned in the flesh would live up to her image of him.

"Well," Claudia continued, "I'd hate for him to have to rent a car when mine is sitting there not being used. Car rentals are so expensive."

"That's true." Julie didn't understand what that had to do with her doing a favor for her neighbor, but she assumed Claudia was leading up to it. Car rentals were high in the islands.

"I was hoping you might be able to pick him up at the airport," Claudia suggested, using her usual method of not quite asking for help. "If you're not busy, that is. I thought if you could pick him up and take him out to the house, he could get my car."

Julie had to bite back a smile when she thought of Ned in his mother's car. Claudia drove a Toyota inherited from Malino Claudia, old and dotted with rust. The engine was well cared for by the local mechanic; still, it looked like something an old woman would drive. Or a teenage boy. Julie couldn't imagine the Ned she'd gotten to know feeling comfortable behind the wheel of her Aunty Claudia's old car. She saw him as a Beemer type-of-guy.

"Of course. I don't mind at all." She smiled at Claudia, not wanting to admit, even to herself, how anxious she was to meet Ned.

"Oh, Julie, thank you so much."

Julie had the impression that if she hadn't been hampered by her canes, Claudia would be giving her a hug right now. Instead, she provided information about his arrival, and Julie promised to pick her up on the way to the airport.

Claudia walked slowly back to her seat on the sofa, where Mabel sat with her sewing. Mabel immediately put her stitching into her lap and leaned over, keeping her voice slightly lowered.

"What did she say?"

Claudia took her time arranging herself, reaching for her own sewing. If Julie came back into the common room, she would see two friends talking together over their stitching.

"Oh, she said yes, just like we knew she would. But then she said she'd pick me up on the way to the airport. How will I convince her to go on her own?" Her brow furrowed as she worked on this problem, her still fingers holding her needle above the fabric.

"Oh, that's nothing." Mabel smiled serenely as she pushed her needle into the fabric, but her eyes twinkled. "Don't worry, we'll think of something."

Looking around the room, her eyes settled on Fred Jardine.

"Fred, aren't you going back home on Saturday?"

Fred admitted that he was. "It'll be nice to be back in my own house, where I can smoke anywhere I want to," he grumbled, his voice gruff. "But I'll miss our poker games," he admitted. "Lot of fun, those."

"You should be quitting that unhealthy habit anyway," Claudia said, surprising herself with her boldness. But she softened her remark by the sincere suggestion that followed. "You can come back anytime, to join in a game. I plan to," she added with a firm nod.

But Mabel had something specific in mind and no patience for sentimental future plans. "How are you getting home?" she asked Fred.

"Ben Mendoza is picking me up. My *hanai* son," he added proudly.

At Claudia's quizzical look, he explained what seemed clear to everyone else in the room.

"Ben is my *hanai* son, my adopted son. It's much looser than an official adoption, a way to become family when you're not blood related. I was a good friend of Ben's uncle and took an interest in him when he moved here after he inherited the ranch. I asked him to become my *hanai* son that year. We had a small ceremony out at the ranch."

As he finished his explanation, Claudia nodded and Mabel rushed forward with the suggestion she'd had in mind all along.

"Maybe we could all go out to lunch together." Her eyes twinkled with the audacious proposal.

Claudia was startled at how easily Mabel managed to do that. She herself would never have been able to impose her presence on someone that way. Her earlier scolding had shocked her with its impertinence, being so out of character. But at least she'd had his best interests in mind. But inviting herself and her friends to lunch! Why it was unthinkable.

Yet Fred wasn't at all offended.

"Good idea, Mabel. I'll talk to Ben about it. We could go to the seafood place and have a nice good-bye luncheon together. My treat."

Amid several thank-yous to Fred, Mabel turned back to Claudia. "You'll come of course," she said. "I'm sure you'll be back in time to go to the airport."

But the mischievous look in her eyes belied her statement and Claudia knew she would not be. And Julie and Ned would be all alone together for his introduction to the island. Claudia wondered if there was a naughty glimmer in her eyes too.

Chapter Six

Julie expected to find Mrs. Smith ready when she arrived at the Hale Maika'i, perhaps even standing by the door, anxious to get going. However, when she pulled up to the Hale entrance, there was no one there. Nor did she find her erstwhile passenger inside, after spending valuable time parking the car.

"Kalani." Julie's voice sounded unnaturally high as she approached the woman at the reception desk. Ned's plane was early and due to land in twenty minutes; she hadn't expected any delays. Taking a deep breath and releasing it slowly, she smiled at the receptionist. "Have you seen Mrs. Smith?"

Kalani smiled too. "Oh, she went with the others."

Seeing the puzzled look on Julie's face, she elaborated. "Ben Mendoza came to pick up Mr. Jardine and he invited everyone in the common room to go for lunch with them. Mrs. Smith, Mrs. Akaka, Mrs. Milho, and Mr. Morimoto all went. Wasn't it nice of Ben to do that? They'll be talking about it for days."

"Mrs. Smith isn't here?" Julie asked, though she'd heard Kalani perfectly well. "I'm supposed to pick her up. We're meeting her son at the airport." She glanced down at her watch. "In eighteen minutes!" Her stomach flip-flopped; she hated to be late.

Kalani's brows drew together in sympathy. "She probably didn't realize they'd get back so late. They were just going over to the seafood place. Maybe you can pick her up."

Julie was already shaking her head. "There's no time." She sighed. "I'll just have to go on alone and stop on the way back to get her. She *is* supposed to go home today, right?"

Kalani looked at some papers on her desk and nodded. "Yeah, I have it right here. Going home while her son is visiting."

Julie glanced at her watch as she hurried out to her car. She wondered what else could go wrong. There was just enough time to get to the airport. The way the day was going so far, she wouldn't be surprised if his plane was already coming in for a landing. He'd be there waiting, wondering where they were. How would she ever explain Claudia's absence?

In counterpoint to the progression of her day so far, it was a perfect Hawaiian day, a glorious beginning to Ned's vacation. As Julie drove along the Queen Kaahumanu Highway, the blue Pacific glittered to her right while Mauna Kea rose majestically into the sky at her left. The gentle breeze of the trade winds blew through her open windows and she breathed deep of the briny ocean smell that meant home to her. What would Ned Smith think of her island? Would he be happy his mother had found happiness here, or would he try to talk her into returning with him to New York?

Julie slammed her foot on the brake as another driver pulled around her and reentered her lane, much too close. Someone late for his plane, she thought, as she watched him turn onto the airport road.

Her heart was still pounding when she made the turn herself. Taking deep breaths to calm herself, she tried to blame the crazy driver out on the highway. But deep inside, she suspected some of the nerves causing her heart to beat too fast had to do with the man she was soon to meet.

For the past two weeks Julie had spent an inordinate amount of time "talking" to Ned Smith. First the emails, starting with brief messages about his mother and expanding to longer exchanges similar to what the islanders called "talk story." Then they'd had those brief phone conversations every day for the past week . . . There had definitely been some flirting going on. Could he possibly be as taken with her as she was with him? She'd know soon enough.

Ned snatched his suitcase from the luggage rack and moved toward the exit. He and Julie had arranged to meet at the curb.

He smiled as he thought of finally meeting Julie of the deep, sexy voice. In the Website photo he'd seen, she stood beside a stooped woman celebrating her ninety-ninth birthday—the soon to be one hundred Mrs. Akaka of course—holding a decorated cake. Both of them grinned at the camera, but there was something special about Julie's expression, a secret happiness in the other woman's pleasure perhaps. It was the glimmer of a smile on her lips that gave him the fanciful idea that refused to go away, the idea that he might be falling for Ms. Wong in a romantic way.

Julie saw him as soon as she pulled into the pick up area. Tall and handsome, but pale, he stood on the sidewalk looking around him, coat over his arm, suitcase at his feet.

As she waited for the car ahead of her to move forward, Julie kept sneaking glances at the tall figure peering up at the mountain as though he'd never seen one before. He had too-long hair and dark circles under his eyes; he looked exhausted—like someone who'd been working full-out for the past four months and was more than ready for a vacation.

As Julie finally maneuvered her car into position next to the curb, his gaze came back to earth and collided with hers. An immediate tremor ran through her body, making it difficult to control her arm and move the gearshift into park. And it didn't help that she found it impossible to take her eyes from his. Opening her door and stepping out, she kept her intense gaze locked on his face—causing her to trip over the curb and almost fall into his arms. Which might not have been too bad, she had to admit.

"Julie Wong?" He walked toward her, dropping his coat unceremoniously onto the bag at his side as he rushed toward her stumbling figure.

Julie nodded, still mesmerized by his eyes. "And you're Ned." Her voice sounded breathy, as though she'd just finished a strenuous activity.

"It's good to meet you. Finally." His smile, the warmth in his voice, the heat of his hand, all combined to distract Julie to the point of forgetting where she was.

His large, warm hand engulfed hers as he took it in his. He leaned toward her, the slight movement enough to throw Julie's imagination into overdrive. Was he going to kiss her? She could feel the heat of his body drawing her inexorably closer. Despite his long journey, he smelled wonderful—citrusy fresh, like limes, perhaps.

They stood that way for an interminable moment, motionless, staring into each other's eyes, hands clasped together. Until the sound of a car horn split the air, startling them back to reality.

Julie quickly stepped back. They were standing on the curb at the airport, more or less holding hands. Silly as it seemed, she was distracted not only by his appearance, but by the warm feel of her hand in his. A strong desire to nestle her head against his chest swept through her. She wanted to know if his arms would feel as warm and comforting as his mere touch of her hand.

His chest looked hard and toned. When did he have time for that? she wondered. According to Mrs. Smith, he spent all of his time working, not working out. Shouldn't he be flabby as well as pale? The Hawaiian sun would quickly give his skin a glow. And she couldn't wait to see his hair lighten from the sun.

Waving away her strange and wayward thoughts, Julie tugged her hand from his. Surely they'd been holding on to each other's hands for far too long. Definitely, he'd leaned in closer after taking her hand. Had he meant to kiss her?

The anticipated kiss reminded her of the ti leaf lei she'd brought. She pulled it from her arm and lifted it over his head, bestowing a quick kiss to his cheek.

"*Aloha*, Ned."

Her lips tingled from the rough stubble on his face, bringing home the realization that he'd been traveling for more than twelve hours. She pulled back, feeling anxious to get him to his mother's so he could rest.

"Ah, *mahalo*."

To her surprised delight, his tentative thank-you for the lei came with an increase in color to his cheeks. So he wasn't quite the suave city boy she'd imagined.

"I hope that was right," he said, the color in his cheeks still high. "They taught us that on the plane. '*Mahalo* means thank-you'," he recited.

"It was great," Julie said, forcing herself to drag her gaze away from his. She opened the rear-passenger side door of the car, and he quickly retrieved his coat and bag and placed them inside.

"Where is Mother?" he asked.

It was the question she'd been dreading. How could she tell him that his mother had forgotten all about him and gone off with her new friends for lunch? But his reaction to her story was far from what she expected.

As she pulled away from the curb, she explained about stopping to pick up Claudia and not finding her there. And Ned laughed.

"She went off to lunch?" he said. "Well, isn't that just like her."

Julie was confused, and more than willing to let him know it.

"It's just like her to forget that her only son is arriving?" He didn't seem offended by this forgetfulness, but Julie was shocked. "She was really looking forward to your visit—it's all she's talked about this week."

"Oh, yes," he said, and Julie could hear the amusement in his voice.

His mother had dabbled in matchmaking before. When they lived close by, she often mentioned to him how nice it would be to have grandchildren, but she'd never done more than suggest that her friend at church had a daughter his age, or a neighbor's granddaughter would be visiting. And he knew that even this new version of his mother, the woman he barely recognized, wouldn't go so far as to break her leg to get him together with a young woman she liked.

With a faint smile he recalled that his mother had been so anxious to see him married, she'd even pretended to like his last girlfriend, a former client and corporate lawyer. Tanya was very attractive, but he'd soon discovered that they were not compatible. She thought in terms of bottom line, didn't seem to mind who she hurt in achieving success, and rarely showed any emotion.

But it was her failure to understand why they had to dine with his mother every Sunday that finally ended that relationship. Wouldn't a phone call be just as good, she kept asking? Her own family lived in New York City and she saw them only occasionally—which didn't seem to bother either her or any of her family members. Just him. But it indicated how much Claudia wanted to see him married, that she tried so hard to like Tanya.

"I'm sure she wants to see me," Ned said, "but she also can't wait to have me married and producing grandchildren. Didn't she ask if you could pick me up on Thursday?"

Julie said that she had; she'd written him that day to tell him so.

"Yeah," he said, his voice resigned. "Then I'm not surprised that she managed to be somewhere else when you went to get her. She had two days to plan. She's giving us a chance to be alone."

Still, it made no sense for her to push him toward her neighbor when he was only there for a two week visit.

Or did she hope to get him to relocate? Thinking of the temperature in Syracuse when he left for the airport that morning, Ned had to admit the thought was tempting. And she *was* his only relative . . . He actually missed their Sunday dinners together, even though they had occasionally seemed more like a duty than a pleasure. Amazing what eighteen months apart could teach you.

"But that's silly. You live in New York . . ." Julie shook her head. "Kalani made it sound like a last minute thing. Someone picked up one of our short term residents to go home, and offered to take him and his new friends for lunch."

"And you don't think they could have arranged that somehow?"

"She did say your mother probably thought she'd be back in time to meet me, so they must have left early."

From the corner of her eye, Julie could see Ned's large shoulders shrug. "Who knows what she might be thinking. From what you've told me recently, it seems Mother has changed in the past year. Maybe she hopes I'll want to join her here."

That was the last thing Julie's dream-weaving mind needed to hear. Big, handsome, with a warm and gentle touch . . .

Tall and athletic, with wide shoulders, Ned had seemed large outside. In the confined space inside her car, his presence was impossible to ignore. It was like having some kind of science fiction force field there beside her. Just the suggestion of his moving to the is-land was enough to send her heart rate soaring. Her hands were still warm from his touch, too, and that warmth was beginning to move out, encompassing her entire body.

Julie was grateful to hear him ask a question.

"What's this?"

Ned's voice managed to pull her away from contemplating her body's reaction to him. If only she knew what he was talking about.

"What . . . ?"

Ned, only too aware of the pretty young woman sitting beside him, making his heart race and his arms feel achingly empty, had turned his attention toward the outside of the car. While waiting at the airport, he'd taken in the beauty of the mountains and relished the temperate climate. But commenting on the weather would be too inane.

So the profusion of words written on the ground on either side of the road was just the ticket. Spelled out on the black lava fields with white rocks were numerous names, dates, initials, and even messages. "*Aloha*" followed by a name and date seemed to be quite popular.

"What is all this?" he asked again, waving toward the outside of the car. "The rocks. The names."

Julie's laughter took him right back to the place he'd been trying to avoid. The sweet notes coiled around him like the lei she'd given him, the warm sound insinuating itself into every part of his being. Once again, his heart raced, he felt uncomfortably warm, and her scent filled his nostrils. She smelled like gardenias, a fragrance he'd always found appealing. Exotic, as Hawaii was . . . as she was.

Ned caught himself just before he heaved a heartfelt sigh. Leave it to his mother to send her alone to pick him up. Unfortunately, she seemed to have chosen well this time. Julie was beyond appealing. He'd forgotten himself enough to hold on to her hand for long minutes at the airport. He'd lost himself in her eyes, as corny as that sounded. If not for an impatient driver sitting on his horn, they'd probably have kissed, right there at the curb. Safer by far to ask about the strange landscape.

"This is our Hawaiian graffiti," Julie explained. "People collect the white coral from the shoreline and bring it here to leave messages. You'll see a lot of good-bye and hello ones here around the airport road. Going out toward Malino we'll see more that are just names and dates, or Joe heart Mary. That kind of thing."

"Amazing."

They drove in silence for a while, Ned reading the names in the lava field to keep his mind suitably distracted. And the warm, sea-scented air blowing into the car helped, feeling like heaven after the chill of central New York early that morning.

But it was impossible to ignore the woman beside him. He found himself glancing at her over and over again, intrigued by her open face and the smile that played at her lips, as though an inner happiness was contained inside her just waiting to burst forth.

"I'm happy to meet you finally," he said, regretting the stilted sound of the words, and making a second attempt that was little better. "I've enjoyed our correspondence."

Julie smiled. So he really did write the way he talked—short and concise. And a bit on the formal side. "I've enjoyed it too. Isn't it funny that your mom moved here because she met my aunty by writing letters? And then we met the same way. Sort of. Not letters, but, you know, twenty-first century kine correspondence," she finished, falling into some island style pidgin that better explained her thoughts.

"It's so beautiful here, with the ocean and the mountains. But I can't believe how desolate it looks. These lava fields look fresh," he added, frowning at acres of black rock on both sides of the highway. "Is it really safe to live here?"

"Of course." Julie had forgotten how nervous some of the mainland visitors could be about the active volcano. It had been a long time since she'd spoken to someone who thought the volcano might be a danger. "Our volcanoes are among the safest in the world. And it's been years since the mountain erupted and these flows came through. This is the older part of the island. Down in the Puna district there is more danger—that's the area near Volcanoes National Park where the ongoing eruption has caused some problems. But it's not dangerous out in Malino. Wait until you see how green it is there. People raise cattle and have large vegetable gardens. It's very nice."

"Mother certainly seems to like it. She always planted flowers in the summer," he added.

"Well, she has them all year round now," she said. "Are you upset that she moved so far away?"

"No. I want her to be happy, and I know she was lonely after Father died. She wasn't really involved in much by then. I guess she gave up most of her activities while she was nursing him through his illness. Talking to you about Mother has brought back a great deal of memories. She used to do a lot with the PTA and the school. And the church. I guess I lost touch with what was happening while I was in college. We're all self-involved at that age."

The miles dropped behind them as they spoke of their college years, and it seemed like mere seconds later that Julie pulled into the circular drive in front of the Hale Maika'i.

Claudia came through the door as soon as the car stopped. Julie shook her head—that was what she'd expected when she'd pulled up an hour ago.

Ned hopped out of the car almost before it came to a full stop. Julie stayed inside the car so that mother and son could greet one another with some measure of privacy. But that didn't preclude her watching. And noting the obvious pleasure they found in seeing one another. There was a noticeable tenderness present in Ned's interaction with his mother. From their correspondence, Julie suspected Ned, like Claudia, was not one who allowed emotions to be seen. Yet he engulfed his mother in his arms, cradling her lovingly while Julie suspected that Claudia struggled not to cry—giving one and all a ringside seat to see the love they shared. Didn't they say that a man would treat his wife the way he treated his mother? Not that she should be concerned with that . . .

By now all of Claudia's new friends had made their way to the Hale entry, anxious to see the son she'd spoken of so often in the past week.

As Claudia introduced Ned to her friends, Julie finally exited the car, popping the trunk for the Hale staffer who carried out Claudia's bag. She noted the polite way Ned greeted the other residents and then the care he used in helping his mother seat herself comfortably in the front seat. Much as she protested, he insisted that Claudia take that position as it would be easier on her leg.

As soon as Ned took his place in the back seat and closed the door, Claudia spoke to Julie, half turning so that she could include Ned in her explanation. "I'm so sorry about lunch. I was sure I'd be back before you arrived."

Julie, suspicious after Ned's comments, couldn't fault the sincerity in her voice. "I was surprised. But we found each other okay, so no harm done. It's a shame you weren't able to see Ned right away though." Her eyes met Ned's in the rearview mirror as she checked to be sure he had his seatbelt secured before pulling out into the street. Ned winked at her. Flustered, her hand slipped off the gearshift.

Julie's parents appeared almost as soon as they pulled into Claudia's driveway. Julie was not surprised, even though they had not talked about it that morning. She'd expected them to come over with Ginger to welcome Claudia home. Also, to invite her and her son for dinner. Which they did. It was the Malino way, the Hawaiian way, sharing *aloha* with a newcomer, helping a neighbor who was temporarily handicapped. Julie was sure Claudia would be sharing many meals with them in the next month.

The invitation came as soon as the introductions were over. And as soon as the exuberant Ginger calmed down. The dog was so excited to see her mistress again, they all had to be alert so that she didn't knock the small woman to the ground.

"No reason for you to have to cook something on your first day back," Julie heard her father tell Claudia. He stroked Ginger's head, holding tight to her leash so that she didn't try to jump up on her mistress and upset Claudia's balance.

"You'll probably have to restock your kitchen," Valerie added, "after being away all this time. I did clean out your refrigerator so you won't have to worry about odors or mold."

Julie thought Mrs. Smith seemed particularly pleased by the dinner invitation, and she didn't even protest that she didn't want to be a bother. Such change in her usual behavior brought back that suggestion of Ned's that seemed determined to haunt her thoughts.

Was Mrs. Smith trying to interest Ned in a local girl so that he'd entertain the thought of moving? Was she trying to lure her son to the island by an attempt to kindle a romance with her neighbor? She could understand a mother wanting her son to live nearby, but it was difficult to reconcile the self-effacing woman with a situation that put her neighbor and friend in such an awkward position.

"I've made up some of my famous teriyaki sauce," Tom said, "and I have both beef and chicken marinating."

"I can't tell you how good that sounds after three months of frozen dinners," Ned said.

Julie decided that made the perfect exit line for her, and got back into her car. She had to move it over to her house and it seemed appropriate to leave while Ned had exposed a blot on his so far perfect image. Three months of frozen dinners? Obviously, the man didn't cook. Maybe he was one of those guys who thought only women cooked. While she wasn't sure if that gelled with the picture she'd formed so far, his last remark made it a possibility. And she needed some kind of blot on his image right now, or she'd soon be hopelessly in love. Their email and phone correspondence had her halfway there, and it was obvious from their initial meeting that the chemistry between them was potent. And he would be right next door for the next two weeks!

"Mother," Ned began, once they were alone together. "We have to talk."

Claudia led the way into the house while Ned controlled Ginger on her leash. Claudia pointed out the doors leading to the various rooms, though she didn't escort him through the house, explaining that she was "not that good with the canes." Then she sat herself on the sofa in the living room, putting the canes to one side so she could give Ginger a proper greeting.

When Ned spoke, Claudia, still fussing over the big golden, looked toward him, then rapidly down again. She seemed nervous. Good grief, he hoped he wasn't frightening his own mother. Had his tone of voice been harsh? He hadn't meant it to be.

"Mother," he began again, this time making sure his voice was light.

"It's really good to see you, Ned," she said simply.

After telling the dog how happy she was to be back, and how much she'd been missed, she probably thought she ought to say something similar to her only son. But he had noticed the way she clung to him during their initial hug of greeting at the care center. And even now, her eyes glimmered with the sheen of tears unshed.

"It's been so long," she added.

Longing infused her voice. Mother inducing guilt— this he could handle.

"You're so pale," Claudia continued. "You should get out of Syracuse too."

Ned lowered his eyelids, wondering if this was what she had planned all along. No, he wasn't going there, not yet.

"Ginger is a nice dog," he said.

They both watched her run from room to room, always coming back to Claudia in between trips, as though checking to be sure she was really there, and there to stay.

"I think she's glad to be home," Claudia said.

"I guess you are too," Ned said. "You look terrific, Mother. Moving here has been good for you. You're standing taller, and I don't think it has anything to do with your leg and the canes. Julie told me you've been playing the piano for the others at the care center. That's a very nice thing to do. I'm proud of you."

Claudia's smile made him glad of his compliments. His mother had always been much too self-effacing, and after his father's death she'd retreated into herself in a way that he feared might not be healthy. Now he could see that her move to Hawaii had indeed been the best thing for her—something he'd long believed, despite his initial misgivings, and although he'd had no proof until now.

Still, he was not about to allow her to play games with him—or with her neighbor. He liked Julie too much to let her get hurt because his mother wanted to push them together according to some agenda of her own.

"I know what you're trying to do . . ." he began, noting the innocent look his mother threw his way—right after he caught a brief flash of panic flit through her eyes.

Claudia smiled sweetly, lowering her eyelids. "You're too sweet. You knew I was trying to put my leg up, did you? I could use your help, dear."

Ned immediately went over and lifted her leg until it rested on the sofa beside her. He moved a pillow behind her back, to make her more comfortable.

"Mother, you're changing the subject." He ran his fingers through his hair, rubbing his nape when they reached that tender spot. Whoever designed airplane seats must have worked for the Inquisition in a previous life.

He seated himself on the chair beside the sofa and looked directly into his mother's face. "I'm talking about that little maneuver of yours to get Julie and I alone together. You've tried your hand at matchmaking before, and I wouldn't usually mind. Too much," he added with a wry smile. "But in this case you're way out of line. Julie is a very nice person, and I like her—what little I've seen of her," he added. He knew Julie worried that her initial contact with him could be viewed as unethical, so he hoped to continue keeping their correspondence secret. "But you're not being fair to her. You know I live on the mainland. It's where my work is, my friends." Though, truth to tell, he had few friends besides his business partner, just many acquaintances. Still, she didn't know that.

"Ned, dear, I don't know what you mean. I told you, I just went for lunch with some friends. I thought I'd be back in time, and I'm sorry I wasn't."

Ned regarded his mother's innocent expression and wondered if she'd learned to do that for her games of Texas hold'em.

Ginger rose from her spot on the floor to lay her head on her mistress's lap, gazing up at her with adoring eyes. Claudia paused to stroke Ginger's head and ears, dropping her chin so that Ned could no longer see her eyes.

"I don't know where you get these ideas, Ned. I wouldn't set you up that way. Why we've hardly been in touch lately. You could have a girlfriend in Syracuse. A fiancée, even."

Ouch, Ned thought. That was a low blow, but in truth he hadn't been sharing much of his life with her. He made his weekly phone calls, but they both knew those were due to his sense of duty. Now, sitting beside her, he felt bad about that. And he vowed to do better.

He frowned. "I can see that we have to stay in closer touch. Especially since we don't have any other family. Meanwhile, I'm looking forward to our visit, to getting to know you again. You've changed since your move here, and that's a good thing. And it's time I got to know the new you."

He noticed that she didn't deny his statement.

"So . . ." He settled back comfortably into his chair. "Tell me about your life in Malino."

"So, what was your impression of Claudia's son?" Valerie asked.

Julie and her mother stood at the kitchen counter working together on dinner preparations.

Julie removed a knife from the drawer and lined up a tomato for slicing. "He seems very nice."

Valerie turned slightly to stare at her daughter, though her arm continued stirring the pot of chili. "He seems nice? What kind of answer is that?"

Julie tried to laugh, but Ned aroused such complicated feelings in her, she found it impossible to turn the question away with humor. And she didn't know how to reply. Even to such innocent queries as her mother's. She'd rather not talk about him at all until she had time to mull over the day in the privacy of her own room. She'd presented leis to plenty of men in the past and she'd *never* had a reaction like today's. The tingling in her lips that came from the light stubble on his cheek had lasted until they were out on the main highway. In fact, just thinking about it now made her lips tingle in that same delicious manner. And the way she'd been mesmerized looking into his eyes. She'd been drawn toward him and thought he'd felt the same strange pull.

Catching herself just before she sliced the end of her finger along with the tomato, she laid the knife down and turned toward her mother.

"Well, he's tall and he's good looking. He looks like an athlete, which surprised me. Mrs. Smith always says how dull he is because he's an accountant and all he does is work. But you saw him, he must work out too."

"Well, you can't work all the time," Valerie said. "And he's smart enough to know exercise is important to both physical and mental health."

"I didn't say he wasn't smart. I'm just not sure what I think of him yet. Maybe preconceived notions formed from what Mrs. Smith has said won't apply. He doesn't wear glasses, like in that photo she has in her family room."

Valerie put the cover on the pot and turned the heat down to its lowest setting. "He probably wears contacts now."

Julie nodded. As she arranged the tomato slices against the lettuce leaves, she added another item to the con side of the column in her mental list of Ned's attributes. Number one, doesn't cook. Number two, vain about his looks. If she could manage to balance both columns, perhaps she'd be able to make it through these next two weeks unscathed.

"Of course that's no longer a vanity issue," Valerie continued. "Most people can see better with contacts, so it's more practical than anything. He might play handball or basketball, and then he'd really need them."

Hmm. Only two items in the debit column regarding Ned and her mother was already demolishing one of them. Scratch vanity.

Julie glanced up. The window over the counter looked out toward Claudia's house and the subject of their discussion had just stepped out the door, followed by an excited Ginger. Ned stood to one side, his hand outstretched, apparently waiting for his mother while Ginger ran in wide circles between the two houses.

"Here he is now. They must be on their way over."

They heard a car engine before they saw Kevin's SUV pull into their driveway.

"Oh, good, and here's Abby and Kevin," Julie said.

Julie could see Abby waving toward Mrs. Smith even before she exited the car.

"It was a good idea asking them," Valerie said. "Ned should meet someone his age. I told Lono to stop by too. He's working tonight, but he'll come by to eat." Lono, a police officer in Malino, was a cousin of Valerie's and in his late twenties.

Julie didn't have any time to think after that, not until she climbed into the shower many hours later.

The small dinner had become a party, with lots of food and good conversation. Lono stopped by for his dinner break. Neighbors dropped in to say hello, bringing more food to add to the already overflowing spread on the table. Ukuleles and guitars appeared and music filled the night. It was a warm island welcome, a complement to both Claudia and her son. There were a few times when Julie thought he looked overwhelmed, but he was probably just tired after his long day traveling.

Ned and Kevin hit it off and made plans to go deep sea fishing on Kevin's next day off. Lono promised to take him spear fishing if they could coordinate times.

Claudia glowed with happiness at having her son there, meeting all of her new friends. As they listened to the impromptu concert, Claudia asked Abby if she would give her an appointment for the day the men went fishing. "I think I'll take you up on that suggestion you made once, Abby," she said, "to get my hair colored. Ned says I look younger," she added with a mischievous twinkle. "Just hearing him say it makes me feel twenty years younger. Might as well look it too."

Abby and Julie laughed with delight.

"You'll love it," Abby promised. "And Ned will too."

"You'll have to bring him over to the Hale one afternoon," Julie said, "and show him how you lead the sing-a-longs."

"Yes," came a masculine voice from behind her, and Julie jumped half out of her chair.

"Sorry," Ned apologized. "Didn't mean to startle you. But I would like a chance to visit your friends there, Mother."

"Maybe he could come to Mabel's birthday party," Claudia suggested. "Would that be all right, Julie?"

"Sure. It's on Thursday," she told Ned.

"Great. Mother was telling me about it," he said. "Kevin and I are going deep sea fishing on Wednesday. I'll probably be grateful for a quiet activity the next day."

Chapter Seven

Time passed quickly with Ned in town. Julie saw him every day, as the Smiths and the Wongs continued to gather for evening meals together. Ned lost no time replacing his mother's small hibachi, inherited from her former roommate, with a state-of-the-art barbeque grill he picked up at the Home Depot in Kona. Then he insisted on alternating the cooking, thanking the Wongs for helping his mother but resolute about being able to do his part.

Julie was forced to move another debit into the plus column, even as Ned continued to claim he did not cook.

"Cooking is done in a kitchen on a stove," he insisted. "I just barbeque."

Still, it was amazing what he could do on a grill.

"He's a good man." Julie's father said one night, as

119

they returned to their own home after another wonderful dinner at the Smith's.

"He'll make someone a good husband," her mother agreed, throwing a meaningful look toward Julie.

Julie, busy looking back on the evening, trying to analyze what it all might meant, didn't notice her mother's innuendo.

The night's meal had consisted of grilled steaks and corn on the cob, served with potatoes baked in the coals. Claudia, declaring that she was not completely helpless, contributed a tossed salad and dessert.

As they finished the main meal out on the lanai, Claudia sent Ned into the house for the glass casserole dish she'd kept warm in the oven.

"I made bread pudding," Claudia said. "And don't forget the vanilla ice cream," she called after him. "It's Häagen-Daz," she confided with a mischievous smile.

As Ned returned and began spooning out servings for everyone, Claudia speared Julie with a severe look. "And you are not to tell my doctor about this, young lady," she said. "It's Ned's favorite dessert, and I plan to indulge as well. With ice cream, too."

"Bread pudding is Ned's favorite dessert?" Valerie said, with a significant look over at her daughter. "It's Julie's favorite too. Did you put in raisins?"

"Of course." Claudia looked offended that she even asked.

Julie moaned to herself. She was still keeping a mental pro-and-con list, but so far everything was going into the first column. The man was human, he had to have *some* faults. But so far, she hadn't uncovered any. And now, it turned out they shared the same favorite dessert. And not even one of the usual favorites, not chocolate cake, or banana cream pie, or even strawberry shortcake. No, they had to both be nuts about a homey comfort food like bread pudding. With raisins. Julie realized that in their email discussion of favorite foods, they'd neglected to mention desserts, only listing favorite entrees and snack foods.

Julie accepted her dish of warm pudding topped with melting ice cream and immediately dipped her spoon in. One bite and she was moaning with pleasure, a sound she realized was echoed by Ned on her right.

"This is so good, Mrs. Smith," she said. Just as Ned spoke.

"Wonderful, Mother. Delicious."

Ned's voice wrapped around Julie like a favorite sweater. And with his large frame so close to her, she could feel his bodily warmth seeping into her, slipping outward into her limbs.

A second spoonful of dessert made her shiver from the almost overwhelming onslaught of pleasant sensations.

Oh, boy, Julie thought. She was in big trouble.

Abby was surprised to see Julie on Tuesday afternoon. She'd been reaching for the doorknob, on her way to aerobics class, when Julie pushed it open and walked in.

"I didn't think I'd be seeing you at aerobics class while Ned is in town."

Julie looked up from her squatting position on the floor where she was greeting an excited Mano. "Why ever not? I'm just late because a phone call kept me."

She straightened up, finally, walking farther into the room. "Besides, I really need to work out after the big meals we've been having. Last night we had bread pudding with Häagen-Daz vanilla on top for dessert."

Abby grinned. "Your favorite. Did you have seconds?"

Julie groaned. "Unfortunately, I did. And you'll never guess . . . Bread pudding is Ned's favorite dessert too."

"Good grief," Abby said. "It must be karma or something. You two, I mean."

"Don't you start too," Julie said.

Abby readjusted her exercise bag on her shoulder and headed out the door. "I don't mean anything," she assured her friend. "I just thought you'd be going straight home while he was visiting, to help keep him entertained. You know, someone more his age."

"I'm not quite his age, thank you very much. I'll have you know I'm several years younger."

Abby laughed as she locked the door and pocketed her keys. "Yeah. What was it, eight years?"

"Please," Julie said. "Between Mrs. Smith and my mother I feel as if everyone is watching our every move, wondering if we're going to be attracted to one another. I even got the impression that some of the residents at the Hale are keeping an eye on us. They keep asking about him and it seems to be more than just an interest in their friend's son. It's kind of weird."

"I can see why the residents would want to know all about his visit," Abby said. "There's not that much to do out there."

Nothing except sewing and puzzles and gossip and poker and endless television programs . . .

"There's a lot to do," Julie protested. That's what her job was all about, providing interesting and fun activities for the residents.

"So come on now—share," Abby said. "Are you attracted to him?"

Abby's eyes twinkled, but Julie knew she was genuinely concerned about her friend's well being. So she struggled to give her an honest answer.

"Oh, Abby, it's terrible. I already liked him before he arrived, but he's even better in person. The chemistry is unreal." She paused long enough to sigh. "We clicked right away, staring into each other's eyes at the airport like love-sick teenagers." She clicked her tongue in disgust at herself. "I think we might have kissed right then and there if a honking horn hadn't startled us back to the real world."

Abby's eyes widened at this revelation, then she put her arm around Julie and pulled her close.

"You go, girl." She chuckled. "I'm happy for you. You already liked him. You should go with this chemistry thing. See if it works both ways. I saw how he reacted on Saturday—to the island, the weather, the neighbors. I don't think it would take too much to make him move here."

Julie was shocked, but also enthralled. Could Abby be right? Was there a chance this could work?

On Thursday afternoon, Ned recalled his blithe words at dinner on Saturday evening. About how happy he would be to have a nice, quiet, relaxing activity like a birthday party for a one-hundred-year-old woman on the day after his planned fishing trip. No wonder the women had smiled so enigmatically at him. How could he have known that a birthday party for a one-hundred-year-old woman would be such a noisy, active affair?

Ned looked around. Balloons and party streamers transformed the common room he'd visited briefly earlier in the week with his mother. "The birthday girl," as she insisted on being called, enjoyed making flirtatious comments to the men—from her fellow residents to the teenagers who'd come for the party. Julie had arranged a prom of sorts where Mabel wore a tiara and an old-fashioned lace tea gown and presided over the party like a homecoming queen. She was enjoying herself every bit as much as a teenage prom queen too, dancing to Big Band music with the boys from the high school and every other male who was present. She insisted that as the guest of honor, every male there had to dance with her.

Not that she was the only one enjoying herself. He noticed his mother doing her best to dance while encumbered by her cast. Happily, she'd exchanged the plaster cast for a walking cast two days before, so she was managing better than ever. He couldn't remember when he'd last seen her smile so much.

He had to smile himself as he looked at her new hairstyle and the stylish new dress she'd purchased especially for her friend's party. Overnight, she'd lost ten years off her age—perhaps even fifteen.

He'd returned late the night before, exhausted after a long day out on the open sea. He'd actually had a bite, something that could never be guaranteed on a deep sea fishing cruise. He'd fought for over an hour, attempting to land what their guide said was a marlin, before the line snapped. He'd enjoyed the sport but didn't feel bad about losing the fish. He figured that marlin deserved to live and fight against someone else someday.

Remembering his time in the fishing chair made him roll his shoulders. His muscles ached today, but in the pleasant way that went along with athletic achievement and a feeling he'd accomplished something special.

He and Kevin had a swim afterward, to cool off and relax tried muscles, then stopped for dinner, and visited with the guys at the firehouse. By the time Kevin dropped him off at the house, it was after eleven P.M. He'd entered the house quietly, ready to tiptoe in so as not to disturb his mother. But she was up, and—of all things!—watching poker on television. After Julie's tales of the poker-playing residents at the Hale Maika'i, he didn't know why he was surprised. But he was.

And her hair! She'd told him she was getting it done, but he was stunned by the change. Instead of the mousy gray-brown color and nondescript cut he associated with his mother, her hair was a rich golden brown shining with wheat-colored highlights. The layered cut flattered her face and showed off her hair's natural waves.

And, as if the new hairdo wasn't enough, she wore stylish new clothes. Khaki slacks that fit her well, unlike her old pants that often had elastic waists and sagged around her hips. A tucked-in blouse in a bright yellow print completed the outfit and made her look barely fifty.

After praising her new look, he'd sat down beside her and they'd spent an enjoyable hour watching the poker tournament.

"Your mom looks terrific," Julie said, coming up behind him with two paper cups of punch in her hands. The poor guy looked tired. "Want a drink? You've been doing a lot of dancing."

And Julie had loved watching him. He'd partnered all the Hale residents, and most of the staff. Except her. Was he saving the best for last, or was he avoiding her?

In the next instant, Julie scolded herself for being paranoid. She'd been running around since the party began, making sure everything was ready, lining up entertainment, refreshments. She'd hardly had time to breathe; of course he hadn't asked her to dance.

"Thank you."

Julie's mind crashed back into the present with Ned's polite thanks for the drink. She watched his Adam's apple bob as he swallowed, thinking how pitiful it was that even such a small thing could look so good to her. She'd never found a guy's throat appealing before. She was truly going out of her mind.

"I've been hoping to have a dance with you, but you're so busy managing everything." His smile was a clear compliment, and Julie felt a tightness in her chest. She'd changed into her favorite sundress before the party and she hoped she still looked good. She thought his flattering look indicated that she did.

He offered his arm, leading her out to the small area cleared as a dance floor. She felt as though they were in a ballroom, in formal dress. She could be Cinderella, she thought with an inner smile.

As they reached the dance area, the DJ began a new song. It was an old Frank Sinatra tune, and Julie could hear Mrs. Kahea humming along with it as she danced in the arms of her grandson, Abby's fiancé, Kevin.

Ned's arm wrapped around her waist, and he took her hand in his. It was a crowded, noisy room, but Julie felt as if they were alone. Everything else receded as she relaxed into the warmth of Ned's embrace, letting him lead her through the steps of the dance.

Julie was not surprised to find that Ned was a smooth dancer, moving with grace and confidence. Even in the small, crowded space, he managed to cover some ground as he led her in an approximate circle around the floor.

"It's a great party," he said softly, tickling her ear with his warm breath. "Mrs. Akaka is very happy. This is a wonderful thing you've done for her."

"Even though she wasn't exactly thrilled with her

card from the president." Julie almost winced, thinking of the pithy comment Mrs. Akaka had made when she opened her card from the White House. "We really didn't need to know who she voted for in the last election," she said.

Ned laughed. "She loved it. Making those wise cracks is what she lives for."

Julie knew he was right, but she didn't want to think about it. Right now all she wanted to do was melt into his embrace. His arms were warm around her, his shoulder hard and strong beneath her cheek. She could do this all night, she thought with an internal sigh.

But of course, she couldn't.

The number ended, the party wound down, and then there was cleanup.

By the time Julie got home, all she wanted to do was rest. The party, so long in the planning, had been a success. Now it was time for her to relax.

Ned found her outside around eight, lying in the dark, on a lounge chair on the patio. She had an afghan wrapped around her shoulders, protecting her against the chill of the night air.

And perhaps from the mosquitoes, he thought, as he felt a pinch at his nape and swatted at the pesky insect.

"Hi there. Hiding out back here?"

"Not hiding, no."

It wasn't completely dark, and he could see her look toward him and shrug.

"I like sitting out here on clear nights and looking at

the stars," Julie said. "There's something really special about looking out at the universe. It makes you realize how small and unimportant we really are."

He stepped closer but was hesitant to join her. Would she be offended if he invited himself to her after-the-party party? Yet he did want to spend more time with her.

"Go ahead, have a seat." She waved one hand toward the other chair.

"I'm getting maudlin anyway. It's the let down after a big celebration. But knowing the cause doesn't necessarily help."

Ned lowered himself into the lounger beside hers, leaning back comfortably and crossing one ankle over the other.

"Are you interested in the stars?" she asked, once she saw that he was settled.

"I was, as a kid. Haven't had time recently. And the skies in Syracuse don't lend themselves to stargazing. Too overcast, too polluted, too much light seepage from the city . . . Take your pick."

"That's a shame."

"I loved it when I was a kid and went camping with the Boy Scouts. We learned about navigating by the stars. Great stuff," he recalled with a sigh. "They taught us to find the North Star, and explained how moss grows on the north side of tree trunks." He chuckled. "I guess that wouldn't work over here, huh?"

She didn't laugh, but he thought he could hear a smile in her voice when she replied.

"Well, it might help you find the ocean," she said, "but that's not too difficult on an island."

Ned didn't want to break the mood by moving so that he could see her better, much as he would like to. Besides, the night lent an intimacy to their meeting that he wanted to savor.

"The Hawaiians used to travel all over the Pacific using just the stars," Julie said. "In their large outrigger canoes."

"Amazing isn't it?"

"Exactly what I was going to say," Julie told him with a sigh.

They stared overhead for a while, absorbed by the beauty of the heavens and their own personal thoughts. Ned imagined large muscular men digging their paddles deep into rough ocean waters, gazing heavenward for guidance. He wondered what Julie was thinking. He didn't have to wonder long.

"So what brought you out here?" Julie asked.

"Mother decided to make an early night of it, and suggested I have a walk." Julie could hear the grin in his voice as he went on. "She said it rains a lot, so I should take advantage of such a lovely evening."

Julie had to grin as well. "Our famous Hawaiian liquid sunshine," she said. "We often get a light misty rain that you can hardly feel on your skin. It can be very refreshing on a hot day."

"I think Mother must have known you were out here. She's still pushing us together."

"You really are the suspicious type, aren't you?"

"Suspicious?" He frowned. "Do you think so? Is that bad?"

"Of course you are, and it could be bad. Every time we end up together, you say you think your mother's trying to matchmake. Did you ever think you might be a little paranoid?"

"I'm not paranoid," he said, then wondered. Was he imagining things, or *was* his mother nudging him in Julie's direction?

Julie continued, barely noticing that he'd objected to her diagnosis. "And when I first wrote to you about her broken leg, you suspected I was some kind of scam artist."

"I didn't . . ."

"Oh, you didn't say so, but I know you were suspicious. Your first note was formal to the point of being ridiculous."

Ned thought back to that first email. He *had* been suspicious. But then there were a lot of people out there ready to take advantage of those who opened unsolicited emails. But she hadn't asked for money, and she seemed to know his mother . . .

He sighed. "Okay, I might have been suspicious. I thought I was being cautious, but it could amount to the same thing."

"Semantics," she said, and he saw her hand wave through the air. "Don't worry about it. I liked the person who eventually emerged from those first stilted emails."

"You did? You do?"

This time he did look over her way. It was amazing how well you could see once your eyes became accustomed to the darkness. She was still staring up at the night sky, a black bowl filled with bright twinkling lights. It was worth looking at, too. He'd never seen such a glorious night sky.

"Um hmm. You're a nice guy, Ned. I like you. I don't know why you always think your mom is trying to fix you up. You're a great looking guy and pretty nice, once you loosen up. You should have lots of women fawning over you. Why do you think she's trying to find someone for you? Don't you think she would have confidence in your ability to do it for yourself?"

Ned took his time answering. Julie thought he was a great looking guy. And pretty nice. Her words echoed through his mind.

She liked him.

Inside he was singing. But he could set her straight in one area.

"There aren't a lot of women fawning over me. Wherever would you get an idea like that?"

"Oh, I don't know."

He could see her gesture with her hands once again. She was ticking off her comments, one finger at a time.

"You're tall, you're good looking. You have a good, steady job. You're a great cook, even if you refuse to admit that you cook at all. I could easily imagine women tripping over themselves trying to get close to you."

Ned didn't respond immediately, mulling over her impression of him. He felt a warmth deep in his chest that she found him so appealing. No one had ever called him a stud before—not that she had, but she was implying it.

"I don't date much, which Mother knows. I work a lot, so there isn't a lot of opportunity to meet people."

"But surely the rest of the year isn't as busy as these first few months."

"No, but when you're in business for yourself, you have to work hard."

"Well, I hate to tell you this, because it might make you even more paranoid."

Julie paused, and Ned wondered what she could possibly have to say.

"My mom made some comments about you. Like she was hinting to me that you'd make a great husband."

"What?" He was surprised, and probably sounded it. "Ah, I'm flattered of course . . ."

He heard Julie's soft chuckle. "Didn't you know you're every mother's dream catch? A CPA. Good job. Nice to look at. Polite. Treats his mother well."

He didn't know what to say and ended up repeating himself. "I'm flattered," he said again.

"Yep, she was hinting about you and I," Julie continued. "Fishing around, trying to see what I thought of you. 'Isn't he good looking?' that kind of thing. I was surprised. I had to remind her that you're from the mainland—from the east coast at that."

Ned swallowed, trying hard to regain his self-possession.

"So, what did you say? To her fishing expedition?"

It was Julie's turn to be surprised. He really didn't know how appealing he was to the opposite sex.

She tried hard not to sigh. Modesty. Another one for the plus column. It continued to grow while the negative side remained glaringly empty.

But what could she say about her mother and her hints?

Should she just make a joke about it? Or tell him the truth? That she didn't know what she thought, because her emotions were all mixed up since he'd arrived?

Making a joke seemed the safest route. So she laughed. "Told her you were the ugliest *haole* I'd ever seen."

She heard him join in her laughter.

They sat silently for a while, looking up at the stars. She pointed out the few stars she knew by name, and he showed her a few others. The quiet darkness, the scent of gardenias and jasmine on the night air, brought a peaceful intimacy to their *lanai*. Julie felt able to broach a subject she would never bring up in bright daylight.

"Have you ever been serious about a woman?"

Her voice was soft, as though she felt embarrassed to be asking. Ned suspected that the enveloping darkness made the personal question easier. But he decided he didn't mind. It meant it would be possible for him to ask about her private life. And, with Julie, he found sharing information about himself easy.

"Just once, in college actually. But I wasn't ready to settle down yet. I knew I would never be comfortable unless I was also fiscally responsible." There was a brief pause before he continued. "Then there was someone just before Mother left. She was a lawyer and we seemed to have a lot in common. I liked her and thought things might work out for us. Until I got to know her better." He took his right ankle off his left, straightened his legs, then crossed his left ankle over his right. "Mother never liked her, though she pretended to. Maybe I should have respected her opinion more."

Julie didn't comment and Ned let the silence take them again. The evening hush was broken only by an occasional car passing on the road and the sound of the tree frogs. His mother had told him that the noisy frogs were a recent addition to the islands, stealing in on some plants imported from the Caribbean. Many people found their loud mating call irritating, she'd told him, but Ned didn't mind it. From now on, memories of the coqui's call would always bring back this pleasant time with Julie.

"So, how about you?" Ned finally asked. "Any serious relationships in your past?"

He could hear her sigh, heavy in the night air.

"I was engaged for a while. Lenny."

Her voice sounded wistful. Ned's heart went out to her, because he could already tell this wasn't a happy story.

"One day he decided to follow some friends of his to Las Vegas. They said the job situation out there was great. He did ask me to join him, but I couldn't imagine leaving Malino. I'm not a city person. And the thought of living in Vegas . . ." Her chair rattled gently as she shuddered. "Not for me. He's been gone over a year now," she added.

Ned almost nodded. He suspected this related to earlier comments she'd made about young people who left Malino seeking bigger things.

"Is he still there?"

"Oh, yes. I doubt he'll come back. He loves the bright lights and the ability to go somewhere at two in the morning."

"Yeah, even on our brief acquaintance, I know that wouldn't appeal to you," Ned said. "Doesn't appeal to me either."

Julie sighed softly as another item went into the plus column.

As they returned to their quiet contemplation of the night sky, Julie realized how much she was enjoying this. Just the two of them, the scents of a tropical night, and the familiar night sounds. It was nice not to have to think of something interesting to say every minute. She and Lenny had never enjoyed this kind of tranquil time together.

She heard Ned clear his throat, and wondered what he would ask this time. She knew there was a question coming, and something personal.

"Have you ever been to the mainland, Julie?"

"No." Well, that was an easy one, she thought. "I'm a small-town girl, pretty boring really. I've never been anywhere, except Maui and Honolulu. Maui is nice, but I wouldn't care to live in Honolulu. It's a big city, with high-rise buildings, but I'm sure it can't compare to a mainland city."

"Don't you want to see the mainland?"

Julie thought it over. "A short visit, maybe. When I was young, I wanted to go—to Disneyland, of course. But I didn't have the opportunity then, and as I got older I realized how special Malino is."

She didn't look over at him, but she was almost sure he was nodding his agreement. She had heard him speak of the friendliness of Malino, and how grateful he was for the way they'd all adopted his mother.

"Unlike a lot of Malino young people," she said, "I've never wanted to live on the mainland. But a lot of islanders do. And a lot more just end up there after college because they can't find jobs here. Lenny said there's a lot of Hawaiians in Vegas. They have local eateries and *Aloha* Festivals and *hula* competitions and everything."

"That's an interesting change from the islands," Ned commented. "The desert, the heat . . ."

"I guess. Though we have our desert areas right here on the Big Island. But Vegas has what's hard to come by here—jobs. Lots of jobs."

"Not only small towns have that problem," he said. "The nice thing about my business is that it's all done on computers. I could work anywhere, really, but I've never thought of leaving Syracuse. I have a partner there, and a wonderful secretary who sometimes thinks she's my mother."

"Are you thinking of relocating?" Julie was amazed. There hadn't been any indication earlier, when he was complaining about his mother's hints.

"Oh, I have to admit it's tempting. The weather here

is so beautiful. But I don't believe in doing things on impulse."

Julie heard his soft chuckle. No, one thing she'd learned about Ned, he would never be impulsive, especially about major life-affecting decisions.

"Though look at my life and my mother's. She chucked everything on what I thought was an impulse, and moved over here. And she's never been happier. All I do is work and nuke frozen meals for dinner. I hadn't even considered whether or not I was happy until I got here."

Julie was determined not to try and influence any decision he tried to make as far as relocating, so she remained silent. The thought, however, made her heart race. She tried to tell herself she was just interested in Claudia's happiness, but she knew she was only fooling herself.

Despite the afghan, the cold was beginning to seep into her pores and she knew she would have to go inside soon. A hot shower was beginning to look better and better.

"Cold?"

Without waiting for her reply, Ned rose from his chair and slipped onto hers. His arm snaked around her, pulling her close to his side. Heat flooded her body, and she said a silent prayer for the solidity of their lounge chairs that allowed two to sit on a single one.

"How's that?"

Julie wasn't sure she could talk at all with the way her emotions were see-sawing at the moment. Along with the warmth he'd provided had come a soaring heart rate, a tingling up her arms and legs, and a tightness in her chest and throat that might preclude speaking.

But when she finally made the attempt, she found that she could not only speak, but actually sound normal.

"It's great. I'm warm now." Too warm, but he needn't know that.

There was another pause in the conversation, that lengthened to the point where Julie felt ready to blurt something out just to break it. Then Ned spoke again.

"What are you doing on Saturday?"

His question caught her off guard. "Saturday? During the day?"

"Yes. Mother and I have been driving around. She's showing me the island you know. We went by that beach, Hapuna. You mentioned it in your email, too, and it's as beautiful as your description. I'd like to spend some time there, get some sun, just relax, maybe do some swimming. But obviously, Mother can't manage on a beach with her leg in a cast. And I'd much rather spend the time there with a pretty woman like you, rather than Kevin or Lono. No offense to either of them," he added, "but you are so much nicer to look at."

He rolled onto his side, so that he could look down into her face when she answered. "So, what do you think?"

"A day at the beach." She swallowed as a flock of butterflies began to flutter inside her. It was the fantasy she'd had, back when they were still emailing—she and Ned sunning themselves at Hapuna Beach.

"Just you and me?" she asked.

"You could ask Kevin and Abby. I just didn't want to spend the day with the guys if I could have a beautiful woman instead."

"Sounds terrific."

Julie was grateful for the darkness. She didn't want to be too enthusiastic, but she couldn't hold in her smile. Was she fooling herself, thinking she was still trying to decide just what she thought about this man? Every time she tried to analyze her feelings, she gave up, because they were way too close to what she thought of as love. And *that* made her very uncomfortable. Which was another clue, wasn't it?

She'd thought she was in love with Lenny, whom she'd known for years, and look how that turned out. She couldn't possibly be in love with someone she'd known for three weeks—and only actually met seven days ago. But more and more, she actually thought she could.

Chapter Eight

Saturday was a picture-perfect beach day. The sun shone in a clear blue sky and the ocean rippled gently, calm and blue. Abby had to work, and Kevin had promised to help a friend repair a corral gate, so Julie found herself alone with Ned. Not such a bad thing, Julie thought, as she peeked over at Ned, sitting on a towel, applying sunscreen to his arms. The careful-accountant part of his personality was showing, Julie thought, stifling a smile. He'd been in the islands for a week now, had even been out on the ocean for a full day on Wednesday, and he wasn't red at all. In fact, his skin had a soft golden glow that added immeasurably to his appeal, and his hair had lightened, acquiring several streaks of gold. Be still my heart, Julie thought.

Instead of Hapuna, which would undoubtedly be crowded on a Saturday, Julie took him to Kauna'oa

Beach. It was a beautiful cove with a white sand crescent of a beach just north of Hapuna. Because the Mauna Kea Beach Hotel fronted the beach, many visitors thought it was private and off limits. But Julie explained that there were no private beaches in Hawaii; public access and even a few parking spaces had to be provided.

"This will be better than Hapuna because we can rent a kayak from the hotel, and there's a restaurant right on the beach for lunch."

The morning passed pleasantly with swimming and snorkeling and an hour in a rented kayak. In between, they laid on towels stretched out on the sand. Sometimes they talked, sometimes they just enjoyed being together.

Twice, Julie helped to apply sunscreen to Ned's back. She took her time, enjoying the feel of his sun-warmed skin beneath her finger tips. Smoothing the lotion over his back gave her a tight feeling in the center of her chest. Not an unpleasant feeling, more of a breathless feeling of anticipation. In fact, she thought she was enjoying the prosaic task far too much. And did it affect Ned at all?

She looked up at his face, resting comfortably on his arms as he lay on the striped blue towel. His eyes were closed, and he seemed relaxed, almost asleep.

Well, that answered that question, she thought. Her touch didn't discompose him at all, not the way it did her.

But Julie was wrong in her reading of Ned. He was far from relaxed. The touch of her hands on his skin sent his synapses humming. His entire body responded, and he had to exert all his control to keep the relaxed exterior he wanted her to see.

He still suspected his mother of pushing him toward Julie. The problem was that he no longer cared. He liked Julie, liked her a lot. And he liked the new persona of his mother even more. Hawaii was turning out to be the best place for her after all. She was looking and acting younger, had friends who enjoyed her company, neighbors who looked out for her. For the first time in his life, he was thinking seriously about a move from Syracuse. Perhaps Hawaii was the best place for him as well. As he'd told Julie during their late night conversation, most of his work was done on the computer. Physical presence was no longer a given in work situations and he had many regular clients who would probably not care where he lived as long as he continued to provide quality service. He planned to discuss the situation with his partner as soon as he returned.

As the sun heated his back, already warm from the touch of Julie's soft hands, he thought how much he was enjoying this visit. The weather was paradise perfect. He was practical enough to know it wouldn't always be warm and sunny, even in Hawaii, but he had to admit the temperatures were appealing after a lifetime of Syracuse's long winters. And living near his mother was something he thought he would enjoy, now that he'd gotten to know her again. She was his only relative and she wouldn't be around forever. And the fact that Julie lived here . . . well, that didn't hurt.

By the time they tramped over to the beachside restaurant for lunch, Ned felt more relaxed than he'd been in years. And hungrier too.

"Sea air must be good for the appetite," he said, peering at Julie over the top of his menu. She was frowning prettily at the choices, apparently having a hard time deciding. "Everything looks good, don't you think?"

"It does," she agreed. "What are you having?"

"I'm going for the fish sandwich," he said. "I believe in having some of the locally available food, if possible. It's usually the best."

"I'll have that too," she decided. "It sounds good."

Once their orders had been placed, they were free to talk. But Julie didn't have anything to say. She was having such a good time; the day was almost too perfect, too fragile to risk marring with inane small talk. It was easy to pretend they were really a couple, not two people who lived thousands of miles apart. Especially when Ned began to tell her what he was doing for Claudia. It was such a couple type-of-thing to discuss.

"I talked Mother into a new car."

Julie nodded. "I know. She told my mom about it. She was very excited. It's a very nice thing for you to do."

Ned shrugged off her complement. "I'm going to get her a computer and cell phone too. She's still making noises about it being too expensive and too much bother, but I think she'll be fine with them. I've been extolling the virtues of email correspondence."

Julie grinned. "Maybe you should show her some of the poker Web sites."

Ned grimaced. "Heaven forbid! Though we watched some poker on TV the other night, and I enjoyed the time with her. She's quite good at strategizing. I feel like I'm getting to know her, but adult to adult, if you know what I mean."

Julie acknowledged that she did.

"You should show her how to use Google. Suggest looking up something she'd be interested in, like quilting. That should get her hooked."

"Good idea," Ned replied, as the waitress returned with their drinks.

Julie watched Ned spoon sugar into his iced tea while she squeezed lemon into hers. Why was it that men could disregard calories and never gain any weight?

"I told Mother that she can always ask you if she needs help with the computer or the phone. I hope you don't mind."

"Of course not. You know I think of her as another aunty." She stirred her tea with the sliver of sugar cane that sat in the tall glass. "Why do you call her Mother?" she finally asked. It was the question that had nagged at her from the start.

Ned looked confused. "What else would I call her?"

"Mom. Ma. Mama. Lots of things." Julie shrugged. "Mother is just so formal. It sounds stilted, and kind of grandiose somehow. I couldn't believe you would actually call her that even though you used it in your emails."

"I've always called her Mother."

"Really?" Julie grinned. "Somehow I doubt it. I'll bet you did the ma-ma thing just like most babies do. And mommy after that. I can't picture a toddler calling mother."

Ned did smile at that. "I guess you're right. But I have called her Mother for as long as I can remember. I might have heard it on a TV show or in a movie and thought it was sophisticated. Or heard a schoolmate refer to his parent that way and thought it cool. She's never said anything about it," he added.

They looked into each other's eyes, then suddenly burst into laughter. It was just too much to imagine the timid Claudia challenging her son's choice as to what he would call her.

They were still smiling when their food arrived. Both hungry after a morning of sun and exercise, they tucked right in, leaving conversation behind for a time. Silence did not loom between them, but sat comfortably, as it does among good friends.

And Julie could look freely at Ned. She tried not to stare, but she did enjoy gazing at the man across the table. He had changed since that first day at the airport. He was handsomer than ever. And not just because of his new tan and the sun-lightened hair, which had been trimmed by the talented Abby. The bags under his eyes were gone, as were the stress lines that had bracketed his eyes.

Ah, those eyes. Clear gray, they tended toward blue when he wore that color, as he did today. She'd bet that in a gray business suit, with a blue shirt, he'd be absolutely scrumptious. With a wistfulness that bordered on melancholy, she hoped Claudia would be able to entice him to Hawaii for further vacations, because she'd really like to see him again. She didn't dare let herself hope that he might actually move to Hawaii.

Across the small table, Ned was also trying not to stare at his companion, a difficult task as it was a pleasure to gaze upon her face. While not Victoria Secret–model beautiful, Julie was very pretty. He'd bet that most people called her cute, and she probably scrunched her nose up at that and wished it wasn't so. But he felt she deserved pretty. Her eyes were large and tilted like a cat's, but so dark it was difficult to differentiate pupil from iris. Her lips were full, though not artificially plumped as was so often the way with Hollywood starlets. Her cheeks, however, were plump and tinged with pink even on a day like today when he knew she wore no makeup. It was possible she'd started the day with lipstick and blush, but he knew she had not reapplied any after their numerous excursions into the water. So that rose-petal pink on her cheeks and the raspberry tinge to her lips were natural.

Stunned at this almost poetic diversion his thoughts were taking, Ned put down his sandwich. Deliberately, he turned his gaze upon the ocean, to the beach where gentle waves tagged at the feet of strollers and threatened a sand castle being built by a young mother and her son.

Had he and his mother ever built sand castles? He

really couldn't remember. He was already amazed at the amount of childhood pleasures that had come back to him since he'd begun his acquaintance with Julie, but of course they didn't have beaches in landlocked Syracuse.

He looked back at her and found she too was watching the mother and child on the beach. He could see the seriousness in her eyes, knew she would feel the child's pain when the water finally took his castle. Her eyes intrigued him, those dark eyes so filled with warmth and, usually, with fun. He wasn't sure he'd ever met someone who was so full of life, so delighted to be a part of making others happy. She had a lot of empathy too and that was the side of her uppermost now.

"Do you think he'll cry when the waves reach his castle?" he asked.

"No."

Surprisingly, her voice was firm.

He turned back to her, surprised. "No?"

She shook her head.

"You see how his mother is talking to him, gesturing at the water? She's making a game of it. By the time the water arrives, he'll be rooting for the ocean."

"You're here early." Abby was combing out a client's hair when Julie walked into The Hair Place on Tuesday afternoon.

"Things were slow for a change and I decided to take off," Julie said, raising her voice so they could hear her over the noise of the blow dryer. She nodded toward the woman seated in the chair. "Hi, Emma. When's the baby due?"

Emma rubbed her rounded belly and grimaced. "Can't be soon enough," she said. "My due date is May 7. Eleven days. Not that I'm counting or anything."

They all laughed as Abby turned off the blow dryer and returned it to its place on the counter.

"I guess you two are off to aerobics. I'll be there myself in June. Can't wait," she added, as she lumbered to her feet. "I feel like a beached whale." She took some money from her purse and pressed it into Abby's hand as she gave her a hug. "Great job as always." She gave Julie a hug too. *"A hui hou,"* she said, as she walked toward the door.

"See you," Julie replied, repeating the sentiment.

While Abby cleaned up the hair clippings, Julie went into the kitchen to greet Mano. She also needed a little time to formulate just what it was she wanted to talk over with her best friend.

By the time Abby had finished sweeping, Julie was seated on the waiting room sofa, Mano in her lap. She patted the cushion beside her. "Abby, come tell me how you knew Kevin was the one."

Abby hooted with glee as she threw herself onto the sofa, startling Mano enough to send him leaping to the floor.

"Great! Did Ned say something?"

Julie shook her head, petting a still-agitated Mano as he cowered at her feet. "No, but I feel like I'm going crazy," she admitted. "I rubbed some sunscreen on his back at the beach the other day. And it made me all tingly, and my stomach all queasy. It's awful. I never felt this way with Lenny."

Abby grinned. "That's because you were never really in love with Lenny. But you have it bad now."

"But is that how it was with you?"

Abby sobered. "Not exactly. But Kevin and I were good friends for a year, remember. Best friends, even. I do recall how much I liked doing his hair the first time though." Her eyes went dreamy. "I still love to run my fingers through his hair. It's really thick, and feels just yummy."

Julie sighed. "I've only known Ned for ten days." She reached down and picked Mano up, settling him onto her lap once more. She needed the comfort of the warm animal. "This is nuts."

"But you emailed one another for two weeks before he came. You can learn a lot about someone that way. So it's more like you've known him for three and a half weeks."

Julie frowned. "I'm not sure that's a whole lot better."

"Well, it's not like you're going to get married next week." Abby rose from the sofa. "Come on, let's get going."

As Abby grabbed her exercise bag she looked back at Julie. "He's going back on Saturday, right?"

Julie nodded.

"Well, you can keep on emailing. Then it'll be up to you and Mrs. Smith to get him back here."

Julie gave Mano one last hug, put him on the floor

and grabbed her own bag. She waited on the walkway as Abby locked the door behind them, then they started toward the church.

"The thing is, Mrs. Smith gave us a present at dinner last night. A pair of tickets for the *luau* at the Anuenue on Thursday night."

"Wow. That'll be romantic."

Julie groaned. "That's the problem. What am I going to do?"

"Want to know what I'd do, in your place?"

Julie nodded, and Abby grinned.

"I'd enjoy it!"

On Thursday evening, Ned ran the Wong's doorbell promptly at five. Julie, knowing that he would be one to arrive precisely on time, was ready.

Ned smiled with pleasure as his eyes moved from her head to her toes, just visible beneath the long, flowing skirt of her *mu'umu'u*. Julie glowed with an inner delight in her choice of outfit. The half hour she'd spent pulling dresses out of her closet and holding them before her in front of the mirror had paid off. Ned was definitely impressed with her appearance. She'd finally settled on a deep purple *mu'umu'u* in a style that was a long way from the old-fashioned Mother Hubbard dress most people pictured when they heard the word muumuu. She didn't want to feel swallowed up by yards of material, not tonight. Her purple *mu'umu'u* was made of a silky rayon fabric that skimmed her body and showed off every curve. She also thought it one of her most flattering *mu'umu'u*. As Ned apparently did. She'd always liked the way she looked in purple, so wearing that color also gave her self-confidence a boost.

Ned stepped forward and draped an orchid lei around her neck—one she hadn't even noticed he was holding. She was altogether too caught up in his handsome face and the interest shining in his attractive gray eyes. He looked pretty terrific in a dark-green *Aloha* shirt with a pattern of tropical leaves and golden hibiscus. She watched the play of muscles along his tanned skin as he lifted and lowered the lei.

Julie couldn't help comparing the fit, tanned Ned standing before her with the pale, tired accountant who had arrived from the mainland. It was obvious that he'd spent his time participating in outdoor activities. Wait until those mainland women got a look at the new Ned. The fleeting thought brought a tightness to her chest and made her breath catch in her throat. Not that she had any business being jealous of his mainland friends. Not that she was jealous, period.

"Mother assured me that giving a lei to my date—her word, not mine—was the proper thing to do."

Julie had been attempting to avoid the word date herself, but a little pang shot through her heart to realize that Ned was doing the same. She worked to pull up a smile. The lei was a lovely gesture and complemented her muumuu beautifully, and she *was* grateful. She wondered if he knew that a gift of a lei was also a gift of *aloha*, or love.

Before she could thank him, Ned leaned down and placed a light kiss on her lips. "And I believe you gave me a kiss along with my lei the day I arrived?"

Julie nodded, suddenly having a hard time swallowing. Her fingers flew to her lips, touching the spot his lips had. "It's the tradition," she said, her voice barely a murmur.

If he wasn't even using the word date, it wouldn't do to have her turning sentimental. However, just as it had ten days ago at the airport, the brief touch of his lips made her skin tingle. But now that she knew the man behind the kiss, it also made her heart leap with joy. She wanted more of that—and not such quick pecks either.

But the front door of her parents' house wasn't the place for such thoughts. She stepped onto the porch, pulling the door closed behind her.

"*Mahalo*. Though I think leis might be included in the price of the ticket."

She was sorry she'd mentioned it when she saw the disappointment in his eyes.

"But you can never have too many leis," she added hastily, lifting the orchid wreath and adjusting it on her shoulders. She put as much sincerity into her voice as possible; she hadn't meant to denigrate his gift. "It's beautiful, and it matches my muumuu so well. Thank you so much."

The orchids had been strung *Mauna Loa* style; the smaller side petals had been removed and the remaining blossoms strung in alternating fashion so that a flat, colorful pattern evolved: purple on the outside, white on the inside. It was one of the more expensive orchid leis, and one of her favorites.

As they headed out to Claudia's new car, Ned tried not to dwell on the small shock of electricity he'd felt when he'd leaned over and given Julie a kiss. A casual kiss, that had affected him in a most un-casual manner.

The drive to the hotel was a quiet one. After a few words about how they'd passed the day, they both slipped into thoughtful silence. Tension filled the close confines of Claudia's small car.

Julie decided to lower the window. The day had been lovely, with the promise of a cool evening. But it was still pleasantly warm, and she loved the smell of the ocean.

"It will be cool on the beach once the sun goes down. Did you bring a jacket of some kind?" Julie held her own sweater in her lap.

Ned laughed. He was glad Julie had brought up the weather, that perennial topic that filled so many awkward spaces. It was just the thing to get his mind off of her presence—and the open window helped as well. Even over the new car smell, Julie's gardenia scent filled the small car. It was the perfume he'd come to associate with her, magnified tonight by the fresh flowers in her hair.

For this special occasion, Julie had pinned up her hair, accenting the style by adding several gardenias at one side. It seemed to him a rather precarious arrangement, those large creamy flowers pinned onto her small head.

But he'd seen other island women wearing huge blossoms in their hair, some even bigger than the gardenias.

The heady scent of the flowers filled the car, tickling his nostrils. It was a heavy, spicy odor, stimulating fantasies of exotic places and equally exotic women. It aroused Gauguinlike dreams of brown-skinned natives, of waves breaking on coconut palm-lined beaches, of sloe-eyed women sitting beneath waterfalls in colorful sarongs.

Ned wondered what was happening to his mind. He'd never been so fanciful, not even in his younger days. Of course he'd never been to Hawaii before, either. Hawaii was as exotic as Tahiti, well suited to dreaming dreams—at least as compared to central New York, a place he increasingly saw as cold, gray, and dreary.

And then there was Julie. With her golden-brown skin and catlike eyes, she was the perfect model for any ad for paradise. Yes, he could easily picture her in a come-to-Hawaii ad, posing beneath a waterfall, gardenias in her hair, a colorful sarong wrapped around her body. Perhaps the same purple shade as the lovely dress she wore tonight.

Dwelling on such things, of course, was not what he wished to do, so the mention of the evening's temperature was a welcome diversion.

"I doubt I'll feel cold," he told her. Her question might have been about the outside temperature, but his internal warmth had little to do with that. Still, he didn't want to let her suspect the full effect her presence had on him. "Remember, I've just come from temperatures in the thirties and forties. In fact, we had a big snowstorm earlier this month. When I received that first email from you, I was working at home because the drifting snow had closed the thruway."

"I'd forgotten that you just came from the mainland and that it's still cold there." Julie sounded embarrassed.

"No need for you to feel bad about that. You have such gorgeous weather here, why should you worry about the rest of the world?"

"But that sounds so . . ." Julie seemed to be searching for the correct word.

"Selfish?" Ned asked with a smile.

"I guess," she reluctantly agreed.

"Hey, it's not your fault you were born in paradise." He smiled at her, taking his eyes from the road ahead for a brief second. "You might as well enjoy it."

Julie finally smiled. "I guess," she said again, but in a happier tone. "Anyway, that wasn't what I meant when I said it. I just forget sometimes that you don't live here. You seem to belong."

Ned felt his heart expand, crowding his lungs so that he could barely get a breath. "Thank you, Julie." He was truly touched. "That was a very nice thing for you to say."

The *luau* was a success.

Ned seemed to be enjoying himself.

Julie found herself explaining various dishes to him, though she laughed over some of them.

"I've never been to one of these hotel *luaus*," Julie said. "There's a lot of food and some of it is very interesting."

"What?" Ned feigned shock. "You mean these aren't authentic *luau* dishes?"

She shook her head, still laughing over a large selection of pasta salads, which she labeled very yuppie.

She was enjoying herself, just as Ned seemed to be doing. With all the tourists around them having such a good time, it was impossible not to have fun too.

"I think a lot of this is some chef's idea of authentic *luau* food," she said. "There's always macaroni salad at a Hawaiian feast, and sometimes there are potatoes in the macaroni salad too. But some of the salads here are definitely mainland yuppie pasta."

Ned ate a forkful of yuppie pasta, chewing in delight at the mix of flavors. "But you have attended *luaus* before, haven't you? Please don't tell me that *luaus* are only for tourists."

"Oh, no," she replied quickly. "*Luaus* are a real part of Hawaiian life. I've attended lots of them in my lifetime. Just not at a resort. Local backyard *luaus*, or the type people have done for weddings or first birthday parties. The first birthday is traditionally a big celebration, usually with a *luau*," she explained, before he could ask. "There are places that do *luaus* for you. You rent the space and they provide the food, just like any other kind of catered event."

"And how are those *luaus* different from this?"

Julie looked at the plates of those around them at the

long table, plates where barbeque ribs and pasta salads lay alongside the *kalua* pork. There were plenty of authentic dishes represented, and she'd steered Ned toward them. But it was obvious that the majority of the crowd was there for the floor show and the opportunity to say they'd experienced a *luau*. And to have a good time.

She had to smile. They were there to have a good time too.

"You mean besides the fact that there aren't five hundred people there?"

"Besides that." Ned smiled too, glancing around the lawn. "And I think it's more like four hundred."

"I guess the main difference is that everyone knows everyone. And backyard *luaus* are potluck—everyone contributes food."

Ned took a sip of the rather sweet fruit punch. "What kind of food?"

"Anything and everything, really. Let's see, I think of *luau* food as the *kalua* pig, of course." She ticked the items off on her fingers as she named them. "And *laulau, lomi* salmon, poi, sweet potatoes, rice, sashimi, *haupia.* There's usually a lot of shellfish and *limu*, or seaweed, things that people have gathered at the shore and bring to share."

She pointed at the dishes that were represented on their plates. *Kalua* pork, the poi, which Ned had tasted and quickly offered to her, the *lomi* salmon in its little cup.

"They don't serve things that they think the mainland

people won't like, like *opihi*. Those are shellfish that some cousin will usually collect from the rocks at the shore, and you eat them raw, sort of like oysters. The *lomi* salmon is raw too, but I guess it's similar enough to lox that they think people will like it. *Lomi* means rub and the salmon is rubbed with the spices—that's how it gets its name. *Laulau* is always served at our *luaus,* but most mainlanders don't care for it. *Laulau* are the taro leaves, and they're wrapped around some pieces of pork and fish and then baked in the *imu* with the pig."

"Fascinating."

Ned was watching her lips move as she talked, his plate of food largely forgotten on the table. What lovely lips she had, still a rosy pink even after the meal which had probably eliminated her lipstick.

"Sashimi is popular with anyone who likes sushi bars," she continued, unaware of Ned's scrutiny as she pointed to a slice of raw *ahi*, or yellowfin tuna. "Not everyone likes the *haupia*," she said. "That's coconut pudding, and I do love it. Though I've never seen it with chocolate and caramel dribbled over the top like this."

Her gaze finally moved to his eyes as she urged him to try the dessert that looked like milky white Jello. And it did indeed have random threads of chocolate and caramel decorating the top.

As she lifted the small square to his lips, something made her falter. She stared at him for a moment, her hand stilled a foot above the tabletop, and cleared her throat in a way that made Ned think she was nervous.

So perhaps he wasn't alone in feeling that chemistry between them.

Before she could pull her hand back, Ned reached for her wrist and brought the bit of *haupia* to his mouth. As his lips closed over the square of creamy pudding, he released her hand and she dropped it rapidly into her lap.

Ned savored the rich flavor of the coconut, but mostly, he was delighted by her response to him. While his feelings might be confusing, at least they were not one-sided.

He continued to watch Julie. Her eyes blinked then refocused somewhere behind him.

"This is a beautiful place for a *luau*," she said, clearing her throat again. "And, look, the moon is coming out."

Ned glanced around him. Not that he needed to. He was already more than aware of the romantic setting. The trade winds blew through the palm fronds overhead, combining with the quiet susurration of the waves on the adjacent shore. The moon had been hidden by clouds, and the sight of it now was beautiful—half of an almost full moon peeked through several small clouds brightening the odd billowing shapes and making them gleam as though from within. The crescent of pale sand that wound through the rocky beach glowed a creamy gold.

The combined scents of tropical flowers, the salty sea, and the delicious food threw his system into sensory overload. Julie had donned her sweater some time ago, saying that she was cold, but his body temperature just kept rising.

Ned was ambivalent about the seating provided— stackable plastic lawn chairs. On the one hand, he was grateful that there was a natural barrier between them supplied by the two-inch plastic arms and broken only when their arms brushed in the normal movements of social interaction. On the other hand, he'd love to cuddle with her during the floor show, which began as the sun disappeared into the ocean. He'd keep her nice and warm so that she didn't have to keep pulling at the edges of her sweater.

He leaned in until their shoulders touched. Julie may have feared the cooling temperatures and complained of being chilly, but she didn't feel the least bit cold. He could feel her body heat through the thin cotton of her sweater. The gardenias in her hair still tantalized him; the pungent scent set his synapses humming, and pulses of desire traversed his bloodstream. He desperately wanted to put his arm around her but found himself hesitating. He felt fifteen again, sitting in the movie theater with pretty little Brooke Frazier.

The adolescent memory was just what he needed to get him to move. It had taken him half the movie to get up enough courage to put his arm around the back of Brooke's chair, then another half hour to bring it down onto her shoulders. Whereupon she'd leaned against him and put her head on his shoulder. He thought he'd died and gone to heaven.

Ned snaked his arm across the back of Julie's chair,

then placed his hand confidently around her shoulder. She looked over at him and smiled, and Ned wanted to kiss her. But not in front of all these people. He'd have to work on that later.

For now, he placed a quick kiss on her forehead and basked in the warmth reflected from her happy face.

Chapter Nine

"Let's walk along the beach," Ned suggested, as the crowd dispersed after the *luau*. "It's small, but there seems to be a path that continues on past the sandy area."

Julie fell into step beside him, taking the hand he offered. Knowing that the *luau* was held on the lawn, she'd worn flat sandals, so walking on the beach would not create a problem. Still, sand crept into her sandals until she stopped and removed them.

"There, that's better," she said, tucking the sandals under her arm and her free hand into the crook of Ned's arm. "Mmm, it feels so nice. The sand is still warm from the afternoon sun."

Though not nearly as warm as Ned. It was like having a space heater beside her—not that she had a problem with that. She'd loved the casual but confident way

163

he'd put his arm around her during the program. If only the chair arms hadn't been between them; she would have enjoyed snuggling up against his chest.

As they reached the end of the stretch of sand, Ned took Julie's sandals from her arm and knelt to slip them back on her feet. She tried to protest, then had to work to keep her balance when she felt his hands on her ankle. What should have been ticklish instead sent waves of warmth shooting up her leg and into her belly. When he transferred his attention to her other foot, she swayed alarmingly to one side, grasping his shoulders to hold herself steady.

Ned took his time with the second sandal, enjoying the feel of her small hands on his shoulders. He knew she'd remove them once he stood, so, before rising, he reached up and took her hands in his, holding onto them as he stood. They remained there at the side of the path for a long moment, looking into each other's eyes, hands grasped together between them.

Ned wanted to kiss her. Her round face glowed in the moonlight and her eyes sparkled with emotion. Ah, but what emotion? That was the question. He didn't want her to think he was after a brief liaison with a pretty island girl. He knew from stories he'd heard over the years, that many men traveling stag to the islands considered such a thing a vacation perk. He liked Julie and respected her. In fact, he cared more for her than for any woman he'd ever met. Their situation wasn't ideal for a relationship—he on the east coast and she in the middle of the Pacific—but he didn't want to endanger it by doing something foolish either.

Before he could even consider whether or not a kiss would be foolish, however, the spell was broken. A family group emerged from the path beyond them, two small boys leading the way. The children ran around the couple still standing there in a semi-trance, shouting back and forth to each other.

"Did you see that giant manta ray?"

"I bet he could eat a person, he was so big."

Ned and Julie heard the boys' parents trying to correct this misconception as they hurried after them.

Ned smiled down at Julie. "Shall we continue on to see the man-eating manta ray?"

"By all means."

Julie could hardly believe her voice emerged in a somewhat normal state. For a moment there, before the little boys ran past and after he'd helped her with her shoes, she thought Ned would kiss her.

She swallowed hard. Dozens of feelings pulsed through her, all of them confusing. Ned lived so far away. And she didn't want to get her hopes up that something might happen between them, then be crushed when it didn't. That could create problems between Claudia and herself, and she did live next door to her. They had a good relationship, with her filling the void left by the death of her aunt. She didn't want to ruin that by getting ideas about her son. Surely her feelings tonight were just the influence of the beautiful setting—the sound of the surf, the heady scent of the many blooming plants, the romance of a bright and beautiful moon.

They strolled slowly along the path, only stopping their forward progress when they reached the lookout where the manta ray watching took place.

About a dozen people stood along a low black-lava rock wall, looking out toward the water. The stone wall encircled a large area to the left of the path that jutted out toward the inlet. Several spotlights at the base of the lookout shone outward across the water. Signage explained that the lights attracted plankton, which in turn drew the manta rays, who fed on them.

Ned and Julie stood together, Ned's arm comfortably around her. Julie appreciated the warmth of his body against hers, as she felt the chill of the evening air despite the number of tourists strolling about in shorts and sundresses. She settled herself comfortably, leaning against him. He might be an office worker with soft hands, but his body was hard and strong.

Julie no longer felt cold. Ned's heat permeated her body, easily spreading from her right side to her left. She kept her eyes on the ocean, on the three manta rays that circled in and out of the lit area beyond the promontory.

"Do you suppose that's the man-eater?" Ned asked, his voice soft beside her ear as they watched the largest of the sea creatures swim up close to their lookout.

Julie smiled, feeling happy at the private joke they could share—just like real couples.

"It must be," she replied. "It's huge, isn't it?"

Her eyes might be on the sea creatures, but her mind remained on the warm male at her side. Her stomach was full, her body warm and relaxed from an evening of pleasant company, good food, and excellent entertainment. This was lovely. She couldn't remember ever feeling more content.

As the enormous mantra ray circled back out to sea, many of the watchers began to move away. The smaller rays passed through the spotlighted area in larger and larger loops, until they too disappeared. The rest of the observers turned back toward the hotel.

Ned peered into the darkness in the opposite direction.

"Want to continue our walk? What do you suppose is out this way?"

"Probably more of the same." Julie gestured back along the path they'd taken to reach the promontory. "Lots of rocks and *naupaka*, I suspect. But it's such a nice night and I'm not ready to go home yet. Let's go." A glutton for punishment, that was her. Because she knew she felt much too strongly about Ned already, and this romantic setting was just making her see him more and more as a true date.

With barely a gesture from Ned, they moved as one to continue their journey along the beachfront path. Just beyond the path was the high-water tide line, where the moon made the white coral rocks among the darker lava gleam. Julie pointed them out to Ned.

"Those are the stones people collect and use to create their graffiti messages."

Ned had to stop and move off the path to pick one up and examine it, and Julie missed the closeness they'd shared. She was more than pleased when he threw the rock back down and returned to her, putting his arm around her, and drawing her to his side once more.

"What was that other thing you said we'd see? Rocks and 'pa-ka' was it?"

"*Naupaka*. It's the plant," she said, gesturing toward the closest bush along the path, thick with waxy yellow-green leaves. There were dozens of them growing along the way—in fact it seemed to be the only thing growing beside the shore. "Beach *naupaka* is about the only thing that grows so close to the ocean. This and beach morning glory, which is a vine that you often see lying in the sand along the shoreline. A lot of plants don't like the salty air."

She stopped to show Ned the tiny white flowers on the bushes, a blossom that looked like only half of a flower. "There's another, similar bush that grows only in the mountains and has the same sort of half flower. And there's a story about why these look like only half of a blossom."

As they strolled slowly down the path, she recounted the legend of the *naukapa,* about a beautiful young couple deeply in love.

"But the fire goddess Pele found the man desirable, and wanted him for herself. She disguised herself as a beautiful young woman and approached him, trying to lure him from his true love. But he wasn't interested. That angered Pele, and she chased him into the mountains, flinging fiery lava at him. Pele's sisters took pity on the young man, and to save him from certain death, changed him into mountain *naupaka*. Defeated, Pele began to chase the young woman, who ran toward the sea, and once again Pele's sisters stepped in. She became beach *naupaka*."

Julie didn't mention another version of the story, where the woman was a chiefess from the mountains, forbidden to marry a simple fisherman whom she loved. She was forced to return to her family in the mountains, and he returned to the sea. But first, she took a blossom from her hair and tore it in half—a symbol of their broken love.

Julie couldn't help but think of herself and Ned in relation to the two people in that version of the legend. She might not tear her gardenias apart to give him half, but Ned would return to his home on the other side of the country. They would be even farther apart than the distance involved in the old legend. It was too sad, so she returned to the story she'd related.

"It's said that if you bring together a blossom from the beach *naupaka* and one from a mountain *naupaka*, it will make a whole flower and the two lovers will be together again."

As they reached the end of the path, marked by a large, spreading *naupaka* bush, Julie reached out and picked two of the tiny white blossoms. She fitted the two flowers together, creating a perfect daisylike blossom.

"Of course, these are from the same plant, but you can see how it would work."

"A touching story," Ned commented. "Beautiful," he added, his voice whisper-soft but clearly audible in the quiet night. No noisy frogs out here, just the soothing sound of the water lapping at the rocky shore.

Julie looked up, to discover that his eyes were on her face, not on the newly formed flower in her hand. Suddenly breathing seemed difficult and a whole colony of butterflies flitted through the area behind her *piko*. Unconsciously, her hand moved there, to her belly button, still clutching the two blossoms into one.

"It is," she said, her voice raspy in a suddenly dry throat. "A beautiful story." There was enough ambient light for her to see his face clearly as he leaned closer. He's going to kiss me, she thought. And before she could determine if that was a good idea, his lips were covering hers.

Ned smiled internally at her story. So she was a romantic—no big surprise there. He stared down into her friendly face. His protective instincts appeared when he was with her, something that hadn't happened in many years. But that didn't prevent him from lowering his head, touching his lips to hers.

Her lips were soft and warm, tasting of the sweetness of the coconut dessert.

Ned lifted his head, pulling back enough to look down into her face, silvered by the moonlight. The stars had never been so bright nor had a lopsided moon been more romantic. Her eyes held a dreamy, faraway look, as if she still envisaged the legendary couple pursued by Pele and turned into shrubbery. Personally, Ned thought he'd rather die in battle than become a shrub, but that was beside the point.

Julie's lips were shiny, full and still slightly parted. Altogether too tempting. Unable to resist, he lowered his lips to hers once more.

The first kiss had been a delight, the second even better. Sweet as honey, her mouth was warm and welcoming. She melted against him, as if her knees were suddenly too weak to support her slender body. Her hands gripped his shoulders, the delicate blossoms forgotten. Unseen, they tumbled over his shoulder, falling to rest amid the pale green leaves of the bush from which they'd been plucked.

When he ended the kiss, Ned continued to hold her. She tucked her head against his chest and Ned tightened his arms around her. When he felt a shiver tremble through her body, he looked down at her, tender concern flooding him.

"Cold?"

She still wore the sweater she'd donned earlier, but it was cooler here on the beach path. He could also feel the salt spray, fine as a mist in the breeze.

"You taste salty," he said as she pulled away to look up at him. Already he missed her warm presence against his chest.

He saw her lips part in a smile. He wanted to kiss her yet again, but caution won out.

"It's you who's salty," she said.

He couldn't resist the challenge. "Let's see." And his lips descended over hers for a third time.

The clouds, which had never strayed too far from the moon, covered it again. Instantly, the cloud glowed a soft gold; but, losing the silvery moonlight, everything below fell into shadow. Plants and faces, which had been clear and bright a moment before, turned dim and indistinct. Julie shivered again and Ned's arms tightened around her even as their lips parted.

"You are cold," he said. "I guess it's time to head back. It's probably late."

The path was lit by a row of small lamps set close to the ground, so there was no danger of losing their way. Ned walked slowly, keeping Julie tight to his side and savoring every bit of their contact. The sound of the ocean would forever bring to mind the magical moment he'd just shared with Julie.

"I wish I didn't have to go back."

He surprised himself with his comment. Even though he'd considered a permanent move several times in the past week, he had not meant to tell anyone. Yet. But then, he comforted himself, perhaps it would just sound like the typical tourist regret at vacation's end.

"You could stay, you know," Julie said. "Your mother would love it. And accounting seems like the kind of job that's always in demand no matter where you live."

Ned stopped, looking down at Julie.

She peered up at him, but her face was too shadowed for him to read her expression.

"Please, don't say anything to Mother. But I have

been giving the matter some thought." Ned's voice was somber. "My situation isn't the same as Mother's, where she was alone and retired and could just pick up and go. There's more involved than just my deciding to move here. I have a business, a partner, clients. Giving the matter serious consideration doesn't promise anything. I wouldn't want to get her hopes up."

Or yours, he thought, even though he didn't know exactly how she viewed their relationship. Julie was definitely an important part of the equation in any future decision. But he still didn't know whether or not she realized it.

Even in the dimness created by the cloud-covered moon, Ned could see the brilliant smile that erupted on Julie's face.

"Oh, Ned, I'm so glad to hear you're considering it. Your mother would be so happy to have you nearby, I just know it. But don't worry. I won't say a word."

The next day passed too quickly, and then it was Saturday.

Once again, Julie found herself driving to the airport. This time, Claudia was in the car, sitting beside her. Ned had insisted, claiming the back seat would be too crowded for her leg in its walking cast.

Julie listened to the banter between mother and son. Her heart ached—and not because she knew Claudia would be sad seeing the end of her son's visit.

She was tired too. She had managed to find the time to corral Abby, Kevin, and Lono, and the four of them had spent hours setting up a good-bye gift for Ned the night before. She just wished she could see his face when he spotted it.

They were turning onto the airport road when Claudia's exclamation came.

"Why, Ned." Claudia broke off in the middle of sending her best wishes to Ned's partner. "Will you look at that!"

There in front of them, in a place of honor, Julie liked to think, was a large Hawaiian graffiti sign.

"It says ALOHA NED and has today's date. Do you think someone else named Ned is leaving?"

"Stop the car."

Ned didn't say it with urgency, but his voice was firm.

Julie's foot immediately hit the brakes, she flipped her signal on, and pulled the car over onto the shoulder. They had plenty of time to make his plane; she wasn't worried about his being late.

Ned hopped out as soon as the car stopped and stood beside his open door, staring at the white rocks that wished him *aloha*. By the time Julie opened her door and stepped out, he was waiting for her. He tugged her quickly away from the traffic side of the car and pulled her close.

"You did that, didn't you?"

His eyes were full of emotion and stared at her with an almost scary intensity.

"Well, Abby and Kevin helped, and Lono. We needed a lot of rocks."

He took another moment to look into her eyes, as

though trying to read something important there. Then he called in to his mother, still sitting in the car and looking at them with sparkling eyes and questions obviously on her tongue.

"Do you still have the camera?" he asked. Claudia had insisted on a round of photos of him with her, with Julie, with the Wongs, before they left the house.

"Why, yes. I have it right here. I told you I want another shot of us at the airport." She reached into her capacious handbag.

"Let me have it for a minute, please," Ned requested.

When she handed it over, he took a quick photo of the Hawaiian graffiti sign. Then he stepped back, so that he could include Julie in the next shot of it.

When he was done, he handed the camera back through the open front window, then gave Julie a quick kiss on the lips. "Thank you," he said. It was quietly stated, but carried a world of emotion. Julie felt her eyes dampen. She'd done right, getting her friends together to do the sign. She had a feeling Ned would enjoy it. And it looked like it had exceeded even her expectations. He was truly touched.

She scurried back into the car, afraid to look at Ned again in case she began to cry. She did hate to see him go. And she couldn't let mother and son see how distraught she was. He said he'd be back and she'd have to take him at his word. And hope a future visit would lead to permanency.

When she stopped in front of the terminal a few minutes later, she was ready. She'd composed herself, and worked on holding on to her demeanor while she opened the trunk and wished Ned a good trip. She took a picture for Claudia of her putting the lei she'd made around her son's neck. Then they had to move on as a security guard came over with a reminder that there was no parking at the curb.

Julie gave Ned a hurried kiss on the cheek. But he turned his head and managed to take it on the lips. Then he grasped her shoulders and gave her a decent goodbye kiss, one that made her toes curl and her entire body tingle.

He grinned at her as she hurried back into the driver's seat.

Then he helped Claudia into the passenger seat, making sure she managed the cast without problems, kissed her on the cheek, and slammed the door.

It had such a final sound, Julie thought. She tried to watch Ned in the rearview mirror as she pulled away, but it was too difficult. There was too much traffic around the terminal; she needed her full attention for driving. Just as well.

As they once again approached the *aloha* Ned sign, Claudia asked her to pull over.

"Now that I know that really was for my son, I'd like a shot of it too," she said. "In fact, can you get in there too?"

But Julie had enough. She just couldn't do it.

"I'm sorry, Mrs. Smith, but I can't. I have to stay in the car. There's a lot of traffic."

"Oh, yes, I can see that."

She took the photo from the car window and hurriedly put her camera away.

"You can go on now, dear."

Julie felt awful. Now, in addition to pining over Ned, she had to feel guilty for hurting poor Mrs. Smith, who was the nicest woman in the world and didn't deserve such rushed treatment.

"I'm sorry," she told her as she pulled back into the traffic stream. "I didn't get enough sleep last night. We spent hours collecting rocks and setting that up."

"It was a very nice thing for you to do. I could see that it meant a lot to Ned."

"He seemed very interested in the graffiti when I picked him up," Julie said. She swallowed, attempting to dislodge the lump that kept returning to her throat. "He asked about it and commented on it. So I thought he might get a kick out of a good-bye of his own."

"He certainly did. I could tell that he was very touched."

Claudia was quiet after that, and Julie didn't mind. She enjoyed the silence herself, though she spent most of it contemplating the new loneliness of her life. Thank goodness for email.

"Could you drop me off at the Hale Maika'i, Julie? That is, if you don't mind coming back to pick me up later. I don't want to face the empty house just yet, so I'd like to visit my friends. Maybe sit in on a hand or two of poker."

"Sure. That's a good idea. Why don't I pick you up around five and you can join us for dinner."

Determined not to mope, Julie spent the afternoon cleaning her closet. She was ankle deep in shoes and old T-shirts when her cell phone rang.

"Hello?"

"Hi, Julie."

"Ned?" She could hardly believe it, wondering if she was imaging his voice because she already missed him so much.

"What are you doing on the phone?" She glanced over at the clock as she sat on the edge of the bed. His plane should have left Honolulu by now. What was wrong?

Her voice came off as breathless, and she hoped he didn't read anything into it. Maybe he'd think she was out jogging, or just back. But he didn't say any-thing about her tone. Not that she gave him much chance.

"Did you get stuck in Honolulu? Did your plane get delayed? Was your flight cancelled?" Questions poured rapidly from her mouth. She was concerned and couldn't seem to stop herself. Darn. No matter how practical she tried to be, the fact remained that she cared for this man. Really cared.

Ned laughed. "You haven't moved into the digital age yet, Julie. I'm calling from the plane."

"Wow, really? You're calling from the plane? But, why?"

"Why not?"

Julie thought about that for a moment then laughed out loud. Why not indeed.

"I, ah, missed you." Ned swallowed, waiting to hear her reaction to that. Interestingly, her answer was as quietly affirming as his.

"I miss you too."

The fact that she answered so quickly made him feel better. Maybe she was swallowing hard too, or taking a deep breath, but her words were sure.

"It's been great meeting you and getting to spend time with you," Julie said. "I guess there's something to this pen pal stuff after all."

Ned couldn't avoid a smile at her words. Across the aisle, a tanned blond smiled back. She was beautiful, but Ned was not even tempted.

"Yeah, I think you're right. We should definitely keep up the correspondence."

"I'd like that."

"As I was getting a slice of pizza at the airport, I remembered that I'd invited you to join me for an Italian dinner while I was there. But we never did get out for it, did we?"

He heard Julie's laughter, and the sound flooded him with warmth. He reached up, twisting his air vent. Cool air washed over him, but it did little to bring his temperature down. Especially with visions of Julie sitting across from him in a cozy Italian diner tickling his imagination.

"Of course not. Did you see any Italian restaurants in Malino?"

"Yeah, I did notice that Italian restaurants were a bit thin. But there are some on the island. I checked online while I was waiting for my plane to board."

He thought her heard her chuckle.

"Why am I not surprised."

"Web surfing is a good way to spend time in busy airports. Most airports have free wi-fi."

Ned suddenly remembered her early impression of him and wondered if he was being pompous.

"Is this call costing you a fortune?" she asked.

"It's nice of you to be concerned, but no, it isn't."

"Oh. That's good."

Ned had to smile at her concern. The call was pricey, but well worth the cost.

They spoke for another ten minutes—until Ned said they were serving dinner and he'd have to go.

"Mystery meat?" Julie asked.

"How'd you know?"

Julie closed the phone, but the distinct click did not leave her feeling lost or lonely. He'd called her from the plane!

She grabbed a soft, shaggy dog that decorated the top of her bed, pulling it hard into her stomach and squeezing it tight. Her eyes focused on the mess in her closet but she barely saw it.

Not bothering to raise herself off the bed, she opened the phone back up and pushed a button.

Abby picked up on the first ring.

"He called from the plane!"

"Wha . . . ?"

Julie quickly realized she'd gone too fast for Abby. "I just got a call from Ned. Did you know you can make calls from the plane?"

"Yeah, I did. It's expensive though."

"Is it? Darn, we talked for a long time, too. He said it wasn't costing him a fortune."

"Maybe he thought you were worth the price," Abby said.

There was a pause before Abby's voice came back, tentative this time. "You know, Julie, it's kind of boring when you're on a plane. All that time squished into a narrow seat, and some movie you aren't interested in watching."

Julie thought she saw where this was going, and she didn't want to squash her dream.

"Maybe you shouldn't read too much into it," Abby finished.

But Julie refused to let Abby bring her down off her cloud.

"He said he missed me."

"Okay, that sounds promising."

"He asked me to have dinner with him next time he visits."

"Even better. Did he say when?"

"Oh, come on, Abby. He just left."

"Yeah, I know. I just don't want you to get hurt, you know?"

"I know. Just like I know he's too far away to take seriously. But I like him. He's a nice guy. It's okay that we're friends, right?"

"Right."

"Good. Then I'll see you on Tuesday. I'm going to go email him, so he'll have a note from me waiting when he gets home."

Julie hung up immediately. She thought Abby might have another thing or two to say, and she wasn't sure she wanted to hear any more cautions. She was allowed to feel wonderful and dreamily romantic for an evening, wasn't she?

She rose from the bed and hurried to the computer, still hugging the dog to her chest. For one brief moment, she'd imagined that he was back, calling for a ride from the Kona airport. That he'd decided against returning to the east and was here to stay. And what an interesting mix of emotions that had caused! Her heartbeat raced, her throat felt parched, her stomach did a somersault.

Poor Abby was trying to keep her from getting hurt, but she was long past the point of help. It was unlikely that Ned would move to Malino and want to be with her. But it wasn't as if she had given up a local boyfriend to moon over him. She would remain friends with Ned and enjoy the "conversations" they shared. And she wouldn't let Ned stand in the way of getting to know someone local, if the opportunity arose.

Sitting in front of the computer, she called up a NEW MAIL window and filled in Ned's address. She hesitated a moment over the subject line, then began to type.

Ned went straight to bed after his long day of travel and slept for ten hours straight. He didn't open his email until a full twenty-four hours after his arrival home. As he sorted through the accumulation of two days worth of messages, he noticed one that started his heart beating rapidly.

From your mom's neighbor said the subject line.

He smiled at the familiar line. That was how Julie had headed her very first note to him. It was amazing what had come from that one short note. Well, maybe not so short.

He clicked it open.

Ned,

It was so special having you here with us in Malino. Now you'll be able to understand things your mom talks about. And you won't have to worry about whether or not she's well cared for. I already miss having you nearby. I'll never forget our night under the stars, or our walk along the rocky beach at the Anuenue Resort. Please keep in touch. I like sharing things with you, even though they're small things, meaningless in the scheme of things. You can be my own personal therapist, the person I tell my troubles to, and then they all go away.

Aloha, Ned.
Best, Julie

Ned found himself smiling as he read. A sad smile. What would she think if she knew he was seriously considering a move to the Big Island? He hoped she would be delighted, but he wouldn't take a chance on telling anyone unless he was more certain than he was at this moment. Still, he too wanted to continue their correspondence. He knew exactly what she meant by calling him her personal therapist. She functioned that way for him too. It helped to have someone to tell things to, even if that person was thousands of miles away. Perhaps it even helped to have the person thousands of miles away.

With an even broader smile, Ned hit REPLY.

Chapter Ten

Most of the female population of Malino attended Abby's wedding shower late in May. They filled the public rooms of The Hair Place, spilling over into Abby's kitchen at the back.

The teen girls who attended were good about handling the cleanup, and now only Julie was left, helping Abby make some kind of order out of the chaotic clutter of boxes and cards.

"What a haul," Julie said, shifting a box of stemware to one side. "You'll have to do a lot of entertaining, to use all this great stuff you got." She added a box of everyday glasses to the pile of kitchen things.

"Speaking of which . . ." Abby set aside the gift card she'd been examining and looked into her best friend's face. Mano lay beside her, exhausted after all the earlier excitement. "I got a reply from Ned Smith. He's attending the wedding. One person."

"Yes, I know."

Abby's eyes widened. "You know?"

Julie nodded. "We email."

Abby's eyebrows drew closer, a deep wrinkle appearing at the center of her forehead. "You haven't said much about Ned since he returned to New York."

"Yeah, I know." Julie looked down, suddenly feeling bashful. "I haven't told anyone we email every day. And sometimes we talk on the phone. It's kind of a guilty secret." Julie looked up at her friend, a wry smile adorning her lips. "I guess I'm afraid to tell anyone, afraid it isn't as special as I think it is."

"You email every day and talk on the phone too? It sounds pretty special to me."

Julie was grateful for Abby's support and told her so.

"I also didn't want to give Mrs. Smith and my mother reason to start thinking there's something romantic happening. Though every time I see Mrs. Smith, she smiles at me and asks if I've heard from Ned."

"You mean there isn't anything romantic happening?"

Abby's disappointment was so obvious, Julie had to grin.

"Maybe." She didn't see any reason to tell Abby details, like the way Ned remembered their evening under the stars or their walk after the *luau*. "I had a wonderful time with him while he was here. But I know I don't want to move to the mainland. Especially so far away.

And he hasn't said anything specific about wanting to move himself, though he does talk a lot about what a wonderful time he had. And he says he can understand now why his mother wanted to move here."

Julie pushed aside the tissue paper in a deep, square box to see what it was protecting. A clear-glass mixing bowl sparkled up at her. She pulled the tissue back over the bowl and added it to the stack of kitchen items.

"And once he did mention that most of his work is done on the computer and so he could work anywhere in the world."

Abby jumped on that. "Well, there it is then. I think that's a great sign. Emma's husband does all his work at home by computer, and he deals with companies all over the world."

Abby put down the frilly bit of lingerie she'd been examining and looked at her friend. "Do you think it's love?"

Julie evaded the question. "I've been feeling fairly miserable since he left. But I have lost five pounds," she added with a wry smile and a pat on her tummy. "It's not like we had the leisure to get to know each other the way you and Kevin did. You were best friends for a whole year before he proposed, right?"

Abby nodded and Julie sighed.

"Lots of people meet on the Internet these days," Abby said. "Some of them even get married."

"Believe me, I've thought of that. I've also thought

of the way I used to laugh when I heard that someone met a man on the Internet. 'What a fool,' is what I used to think." She shook her head. "I don't know what to think now."

She abandoned the gift boxes and threw herself down on the couch. She snatched up a soft pillow, wrapping both arms around it and holding it close, the way she did with her stuffed animals at home.

"But you've met Ned in person," Abby reiterated. "It's not like he's lying to you about what he looks like or who he is."

"That's true. Still . . ." Her voice trailed off.

"I think it's the same thing as pen pals," Abby said, pushing Julie's feet aside so she could join her on the couch. "Only with snail mail you only write once a week or once every two weeks. But with email you get to hear from one another every day. Sometimes twice a day. It's like years worth of letters in just a few months, so you get to know a person faster."

"Mrs. Smith already asked me if I would take her to the airport to pick him up when he comes for the wedding. She says she gets nervous driving around the airport traffic."

Abby laughed. "You think she really does?'

"Who knows? I told her I would." She grinned at Abby.

Amazingly enough, in Syracuse, Ned was having a similar conversation with his best friend, his business partner Tyler Bellucci.

"You're what?!"

"I told you, I'm going back to Hawaii for a wedding. A couple I met while I was there. He took me out deep sea fishing." He'd told Tyler about his attempt to land the marlin when he first got back. "But I'm thinking of moving there permanently, to be near my mother. She's not getting any younger," he told Tyler, though her recent appearance belied the comment. Not that Tyler would know about that.

"I can do most of my work from there," Ned continued. "Everything is so computerized these days, office location is no longer an issue. And I can come back periodically for any necessary in-person meetings."

His partner shook his head. "If you're going to be in Hawaii, maybe I'll come to you."

Ned wanted to grin in delight but managed to remain serious.

"So you do think it could work."

"Sure." Tyler looked carefully at his old friend. "There isn't a woman involved in this decision, is there? Other than your mother, I mean."

This time Ned couldn't contain the wide smile that adorned his face.

"How did you know?"

"You've been different since you came back from that visit. And not just because of the tan and the new haircut. It's not anything I could really put my finger on, but something about your attitude." Tyler looked him over, his expression serious even though it was apparent that he was glad about Ned's happiness. "You're more relaxed," he finally said. "Maybe you've just been happier."

"It's happy memories, probably."

Ned's chuckle echoed through the empty office where they sat after hours, having this important discussion. Ned thought that the leather couch in his conversation area had rarely seen a more important use.

"I did meet a woman there," he confided. "My mother's neighbor. We've been emailing."

"Good grief." His partner laughed in earnest now. "An online romance. Never thought I'd see the day you'd get involved with someone online."

Ned ducked his head, hoping to hide a sheepish grin. But what could he say.

"Hey, I've met her, remember? We had a great time, and even a couple of real dates. I think my mother was pushing us together, but she called me paranoid when I told her I saw what she was trying to do."

"What does it matter, as long as you're happy?"

Ned had to admit that Tyler had a point.

"So," Tyler asked, "what does your mother think about the big move? She must be ecstatic."

Ned ran his hand through his hair, looking a bit sheepish. "You're the first to know. I thought I'd tell her in person. When I go for the wedding. There are a lot of arrangements to make beforehand. I probably won't actually be able to move until the fall."

Tyler laughed. "Well, you know I only want the best for you. And as long as you keep working for us I can't complain. Be sure you invite me to the wedding, though. I can hardly wait to meet Online Girl."

Once again, Julie picked Ned up at the Kona airport. This time, Claudia sat beside her as they drove into the airport lot. Claudia wanted to park, then go in and wait outside the security area with leis. Julie didn't object. It sounded like a great idea to her too. She still remembered what Claudia had said to her when she asked Julie if she would accompany her to the airport.

"He always asks after you when he calls," Claudia told her. "I can tell he likes you." Julie treasured the comment.

The ride in had been pleasant, the car smelling wonderful, thanks to the plumeria lei Claudia carried. And, in remembrance of their wonderful evening at the *luau*, Julie had pinned gardenias in her hair.

"I hope Ned doesn't think these are too feminine," Claudia said, adjusting the flowers over her arm as they walked to the terminal. "But I do love stringing the plumerias. And my arthritis makes it hard to twist the leaves for a ti leaf lei. They are more masculine though."

"Well, I don't have any trouble twisting ti leaves," Julie said, "but I like to string flowers too. That's why I did the crown flowers. I'm sure Ned will like them. And if not," she added with a mischievous grin, "he's too well brought up to say so."

As she'd hoped, Claudia laughed.

"He is a good boy," she agreed. "And he's not so boring when he's on vacation."

Julie nodded absently, her eyes already on the area where passengers emerged. Even though it was probably too early for Ned's plane.

The past six weeks had been a special time for Julie. She'd written Ned every day and cherished the time she'd spent reading his posts. She read and reread his entries, trying to learn everything she could about him. They spoke together of their likes and dislikes, their dreams and their concerns. And their happy memories of the time spent together—which both agreed had been too short.

And on clear nights, she liked to sit out on the lounge chair in her backyard and stare up at the stars, dreaming of the wonderful evenings they'd kissed beneath those same stars.

Ned had been to weddings before, of course. In the past, however, he'd usually felt uncomfortable around all that sentimental love.

But not this time.

Was it the quaint little church in Malino, where you could hear the surf break during quiet moments? Where the smell of the ocean mixed with the musky scent of tropical flowers?

Was it the friendly atmosphere created by people who'd known one another for a lifetime?

Possibly.

But more likely, it was due to the maid of honor, beautiful in a slim, forest-green dress and holding a bouquet of gardenias. Just yesterday, those same gardenias had adorned a hedge between his mother's house and the Wong's.

Ned decided that everything in Malino was completely outside his experience. Whoever heard of making your own wedding bouquets and corsages? Not in Syracuse, though it was much more difficult to come by beautiful flowers there for much of the year. In Malino it was apparently accepted that women would gather flowers the day before a wedding to provide these essentials from their own gardens.

As Abby and Kevin exchanged their vows, Ned decided he wanted this for himself. Not just being married in Malino. He wanted the entire experience. He, the city boy, found it easy to visualize himself living in tiny Malino. He wanted a house, with a lawn and a garden. With Julie of course, and at least two dark-haired children reflecting her same exotic beauty. And grandparents next door to dote on them.

Although he'd been told that it was impossible to keep secrets in a small town, he'd managed to make quiet inquiries about the local real estate market that had yet to come to his mother's attention. And he'd learned that the house right behind the Wongs was for sale at what seemed a reasonable price.

As he waited with the other guests for the bridal party to finish with photographs, Ned reflected on his plan. He felt confident that he and Julie were meant to be together, but not totally confident of the feelings on her side. He knew she'd had a bad experience with one engagement, and wondered if that would make her leery of another.

So, to ensure success, he meant to create the most romantic proposal ever. He had another ten days in Hawaii. He needed to use his time well.

"Having fun?"

"Ummm . . ." Julie didn't even look up, just continued to rest her head on his shoulder. "It was a beautiful wedding, wasn't it? Abby wanted everything simple, but that made it all very elegant. It was one of the best weddings ever."

"I thought it was nice," Ned agreed.

At that Julie did look up. "Nice? Only nice?"

"Best wedding ever," Ned said quickly.

Julie nodded, happy with this new reply, and returned her head to his shoulder.

"So," Ned began, savoring the feel of her body against his as they swayed slowly on the crowded dance floor. "About that Italian dinner date I promised you . . ."

Julie tilted her head just enough that he could catch her smile. He also thought he detected a dreamy look in her expressive eyes.

"Still no Italian restaurants in Malino," she said.

"Ah, but I've found one in Kona. What do you say to Sunday evening?"

"Okay." She maintained her warm smile.

"It's a date then."

He placed a kiss on her lips, tempted to draw her even closer for another. But, to his disappointment, the number ended and she pulled away.

"Time for Abby to throw her bouquet," she informed him. "They'll be leaving in a few minutes."

Ned watched her cross the dance floor to join the group of teenagers and young women congregating opposite the raised bandstand.

He blinked when he saw his mother and Mrs. Akaka among them. Opening his eyes again, he saw that they were still there. Well, they were unmarried, he told himself, though he had to shake his head at the idea of the hundred-year-old Mrs. Akaka as the next bride.

As the band produced a drum roll and Abby tossed the bouquet over her head, he noticed that the two old women did not even attempt to catch the flowers hurtling toward them. Instead, they positioned themselves behind Julie, going so far as to push her forward when the bouquet made a high arc and almost landed short of the waiting crowd.

He smiled when he saw Julie reach out for the flowers, nearly stumbling as her movement combined with the shove from behind. But she managed to keep her feet beneath her and catch the bouquet as well, grasping the white orchids to her with an exuberant smile of triumph.

Ned smiled contentedly. It was a good sign. He didn't think she would put that kind of effort into the catch if she wasn't interested in being the next bride; she would have let someone else have it. Julie was definitely the type to believe in the old traditions.

As her eyes caught his, he winked at her, pleased when her cheeks blushed a becoming pink.

"We'll be right back," Claudia told Ned as she pulled Mabel toward the back of the hall. "Just a quick visit to the little girls' room before we go."

Once inside, the two women almost chortled.

"Did you see that catch she made?" Mabel asked. "She'll be the next bride for sure."

"I think he's going to propose before he goes back," Claudia confided, lowering her voice. "I was tidying his room and noticed a jewelry box. A small one."

Mabel gasped, delight showing in every wrinkle on her aged face. "Did you look?"

Claudia tried to look affronted but gave up. She grasped her friend's hands. "She's going to be so happy. I don't know why I ever thought my son was dull."

"I've never noticed this place before," Julie commented when they entered the Tuscan Bistro in Kailua-Kona on Sunday evening. "Is it new?"

"When I called about a reservation the person told me it has been open for six months."

"It looks just like a romantic Italian restaurant in a movie," Julie said, taking in the small round tables covered with red-and-white checkered cloths. Chianti bottles with candles in them stood at the center of each table and Italian opera played unobtrusively in the background.

"So, what's your favorite Italian dish?" Ned asked.

Julie was embarrassed to realize that her mind was blank. At least when it came to a favorite food, Italian or otherwise. All she could think about at the moment was the man across the table from her. About the way he made her feel—intelligent and alive. Everyday things seemed special when he was present.

As Abby's maid of honor, Julie had been paired up with the best man for the wedding, but Ned had still managed to spend most of his time with her. They'd danced together, and talked together, and laughed together throughout the evening. And then she'd caught the bouquet. But, the crowning touch had been Ned's athletic leap when he'd managed to grab the garter practically from the fingertips of a teenaged guest. It might be nothing but superstition, but it still made her happy that Ned had put so much effort into capturing that prize.

Her eyes turned to the menu, as she still desperately tried to pull a food name from her distracted mind.

"Chicken parmesan?" Ned suggested. "I think you've mentioned how much you like chicken."

"Yes." She nodded, grateful to him for easing her way. "I love chicken. That sounds great."

"Good."

Ned gestured to the waiter, who was just finishing up at the next table.

But before he could do more than order a nice wine, his eyebrow shot upward at the sight of two new patrons entering the restaurant. Creeping into the restaurant, actually.

His mother and Mrs. Akaka! What were they doing here?

Before Ned could stand, both women moved their fingers to their lips in the old signal for silence. They pointed to a shadowy table well behind Julie, and therefore out of her line of sight, and once again gestured for silence.

Ned quickly looked down at the menu, hoping Julie hadn't seen his initial surprise. But if she had, she showed no indication of it, placing her order then continuing to talk about the menu after the waiter left.

The evening couldn't have been better.

Well, Ned thought, except for the fact that his mother was sitting several tables away making him even more nervous about what he had planned.

How did she know anyway? *Did* she know?

As the waiter cleared their dinner plates, Ned ordered coffee, asking Julie if she cared for dessert.

"I was told the tiramisu is to die for," he told her.

"You must be joking." Julie groaned, but with a smile. "I'm so full I might not be able to walk out of here."

"Don't worry, I'll carry you if necessary." Ned grinned.

"My hero."

Julie used the proper breathily awed voice, like a heroine in a melodrama. But then she sat up straighter, turning slightly in her chair.

"Oh, look, Ned. They have entertainment. A man with an accordion, of all things."

A middle-aged man had indeed appeared, serenading a nearby couple with a soulful rendition of "O Sole Mio" and accompanying himself on the accordion.

"How romantic," Julie said.

Ned was relieved. He hadn't been sure about the accordion, played by one of the owners, he'd learned. Personally, he would have preferred a violin, but you had to work with what was available.

And he thought he could make this work. During their many online exchanges, Julie had told him that one of her favorite movies was *Moonstruck*.

"Oh, look, he's coming over here."

Julie's voice had a happy, expectant sound, as she lowered it to an almost whisper. "What do you think he'll play for us?"

The man began before Ned could answer, likely drowning out anything he would say. So he leaned close to Julie's ear and whispered into it.

"I made a special request."

Julie's cheeks blushed prettily when she realized what it was. "That's Amore," the old Dean Martin song that was sung during the credits of her favorite movie. Tears welled up and she blinked rapidly trying to keep them from spilling down her cheeks.

Ned slipped the musician a bill at the end of the number, then leaned over and kissed Julie. The kiss was light, as was suitable in a public place, but his lips lingered just enough that she knew he hated to pull away.

Julie felt like she was starring in her own romantic movie. She just hoped it had a happy ending.

The whole evening was becoming too much for her.

She gave up trying to control her tears and allowed a few to inch down her cheeks, wiping them away with her hands.

But Ned didn't seem to mind that she was a puddle of emotion. He took her damp hands in his and looked into her eyes.

"Julie, you're the most wonderful woman I've ever met. I want you to know that I've decided to set up a local office of Bellucci & Smith. You're the first to know, but don't tell Mother that."

His mischievous smile set Julie's heart pounding. She wondered if the entire night was a dream. If he didn't have both her hands in his, she would have reached over and pinched her upper arm. Things like this didn't happen in real life. They especially didn't happen to her. A romantic dinner, an Italian serenade, and now a handsome man sharing secrets he hadn't even told his mother.

Julie sighed with the pleasure of it all. She didn't want to speculate about where he was going next. She thought she knew, but she refused to form the words into thoughts, even if they were only in her mind. She didn't want to be disappointed.

"But I don't want to embark on this new life alone," Ned continued. "I'm hoping you'll share it with me."

Still holding onto her left hand with his, Ned reached into his pocket. He produced a small jeweler's box, and somehow managed to open it with just one hand. Julie barely glanced at it, her eyes still locked on his face.

"Julie, will you marry me?"

A bright smile spread across her lips, and a tear slipped down her cheek.

"Yes. Definitely, yes."

After her answer, and another kiss to seal the bargain, she finally glanced down at the ring he'd offered.

Julie found herself staring at a shining gold ring, at two halves of a *naupaka* blossom facing each other to form a beautiful whole. Her breath caught in her throat. Tears streamed down her cheeks.

"Oh, Ned. It's the most beautiful ring I've ever seen." Her breathy voice whispered the words, her voice even deeper than usual. "It's perfect. Absolutely perfect."

Ned's face reddened with pleasure at her reaction.

"I knew what I wanted, but didn't think I'd be able to find anything like it." He removed the ring from its velvet bed and slipped it on her finger. "It's amazing what you can find online these days."

He smiled tenderly at her.

She returned the smile.

"Correspondents," she said. "Life companions."

"Engagement rings," he added.

He leaned forward for another kiss.

His lips had barely touched hers when Claudia and Mabel appeared beside them. He groaned.

"Mrs. Smith. Mrs. Akaka." Julie looked confused. "What are you doing here?"

"Eating dinner, dear," Claudia replied.

"Did he propose?" Mrs. Akaka asked. "We're pretty sure we saw him give you a ring. It's kind of dark in here though."

It felt good to laugh. Julie let her laughter ring out, as she raised her left hand to show off her new ring. A beam of light caught on the shiny new gold and sparked off it, throwing a rainbow beam across Julie's line of sight. It was surely an omen, a sign of the good times to come.

"Oh, it's so pretty," Claudia said.

Julie could see that she, too, had tears in her eyes.

Not Mrs. Akaka. The old woman just nodded.

"Not bad. *Naupaka,* huh? There must be a story there," she guessed. "You'll have to tell us tomorrow, Julie. Come on, Claudia, let's give them some privacy."

She took her friend's arm and pulled her toward the entrance.

Ned watched them go, shaking his head.

"I'm still suspicious of those two. I'm sure they set us up. But I guess it doesn't really matter, because I found you."

He placed a light kiss on her lips then picked up his wine glass. "To us. Two disparate halves, forming a complete whole."

Julie picked up her wine glass and touched it to his. The ringing tinkle of the crystal sang out, clear and bright.

"To us."

WITHDRAWAL